THIS BOOK
BELONGS TO

\- \- \- \- \- \- \- \- \- \- \- \- \- \- \- \-

\- \- \- \- \- \- \- \- \- \- \-

# By the Same Author

Emily Eyefinger
Emily Eyefinger, Secret Agent
Emily Eyefinger and the Lost Treasure
Emily Eyefinger and the Black Volcano
Emily Eyefinger's Alien Adventure
Emily Eyefinger and the Devil Bones
Emily Eyefinger and the Balloon Bandits
Emily Eyefinger and the Ghost Ship
Emily Eyefinger and the Puzzle in the Jungle
Emily Eyefinger and the City in the Sky

Piggott Place
Piggotts in Peril

The Case of the Graveyard Ghost and Other Mysteries
The Case of the Vampire's Wire and Other Mysteries

# SELBY SCRAMBLED

# DUNCAN BALL

## with illustrations by Allan Stomann

Angus&Robertson

An imprint of HarperCollins*Publishers*

Acknowledgments: The author would like to thank Shona Martyn, Lisa Berryman, Vanessa Radnidge, Cristina Rodrigues, Barbara Pepworth, Helen Beard and all the others at HarperCollins Australia, who make these books possible. Thanks as well to Callum and Darcy Gray, youth quality assurance consultants, and to Allan Stomann for his wonderful pictures of a dog he's never seen.

## Angus&Robertson

An imprint of HarperCollins*Publishers*, Australia

First published in Australia in 2004
by HarperCollins*Publishers* Australia Pty Limited
ABN 36 009 913 517
www.harpercollins.com.au

**HarperCollins*Publishers***
Level 13, 201 Elizabeth Street, Sydney NSW 2000, Australia
Unit D, 63 Apollo Drive, Rosedale, Auckland 0632, New Zealand
A 53, Sector 57, Noida, UP, India
1 London Bridge Street, London SE1 9GF, United Kingdom
2 Bloor Street East, 20th floor, Toronto, Ontario M4W 1A8, Canada
195 Broadway, New York NY 10007, USA

National Library of Australia Cataloguing-in-Publication data:

Ball, Duncan, 1941– .
   Selby scrambled.
   ISBN 0 207 19911 6
   1. Dogs – Juvenile fiction. I. Title.
A823.3

Cover and internal design by Christabella Designs
Typeset in 14/18 Bembo by HarperCollins Design Studio
Printed and bound in Australia by Griffin Press
50gsm Bulky News used by HarperCollins*Publishers* is a natural, recyclable
product made from wood grown in sustainable plantation forests. The
manufacturing processes conform to the environmental regulations in the
country of origin, New Zealand.

*To all the kids who have written to me and to Selby.*

# AUTHOR'S NOTE

When Selby rang me and told me these stories, it left me in a state of shock. Just the adventure he had with Dr Trifle's Wall Walkers and climbing the Crystal Tower could have filled this whole book but, no, he was also captured by a robot, he had to break out of prison, deal with the most superstitious people on earth, and then there was that dreadful operation. Quite frankly, after hearing about these adventures, I don't know what to believe anymore.

Anyone who has read about Selby knows that Selby is a real talking dog. But 'Selby' isn't his real name. He made it up. He won't tell me his real name, or the real name of Bogusville, or the Trifles — or anything. When I'm writing the stories this can be confusing. For example, recently the Trifles read a Selby book. And Mrs Trifle said, 'Goodness me' (she often says 'Goodness me') 'that dog, Selby, is a lot like our Selby.' Well, of course their dog is the real Selby and his name isn't really 'Selby' but I couldn't write, 'That dog, Selby, is a lot like our Ralph' because Selby's real name isn't Ralph either. Oh, now my brain is totally scrambled. Anyway, you'll work it out when you read the stories.

I hope you like them.

*Duncan Ball*

# CONTENTS

# FORE

Before you read this book you should know that I am Selby, the only talking dog in Australia and, perhaps, the world. No one in the whole world— except those awful brats Willy and Billy and maybe a few other people who nobody would believe anyway— knows that I can talk. Well, of course, you do.

Anyway, I've had lots of rip-roaring adventures recently and then I rang the author, Duncan Ball, and he wrote them and put them in this book. There are sinking ships, sports stars (me), radio personalities (me again) and stacks of stuff that I can't tell you or I'll ruin it for you.

So grab the chips and dips and start reading! Selby 🐾

# SELBY ON ICE

'A red ship is sailing along and it runs into a blue ship. All the passengers were marooned. Get it?'

Gary Gaggs, the famous comedian and friend of the Trifles was in Dr and Mrs Trifle's lounge room, telling his latest jokes.

'Red and blue: *marooned*. I get it,' Selby thought. 'This guy kills me.'

'Two ropes are hanging over the side of a ship,' Gary continued. 'One of them says, "Are you a rope?" and the other one says, "I'm afraid not." Woo woo woo. Get it: a *frayed knot*.'

'Are these the jokes you're going to be telling on the *Fun 'n' Happy Cruise*?' Mrs Trifle asked.

1

'These are the jokes, folks,' Gary said. 'They're going to broadcast them all around the ship so people can hear them no matter where they are. I'm going to make the *Fun 'n' Happy Cruise* fun fun fun and hap-hap-happy. Why don't you two come along?'

'We could use a break,' Mrs Trifle said. 'What ship is it?'

'It's called the *Rose Bouquet 2*.'

'The *Rose Bouquet 2*? I remember the *Rose Bouquet 1*. Didn't it sink?'

'That's right,' Gary said. 'It hit an iceberg but everyone got off safely.'

'It's very odd to name a ship after one that sank,' Dr Trifle said.

'They didn't name it *after* the other one,' Gary explained. 'The *Rose Bouquet 2* is the *Rose Bouquet 1* fixed up. They just refloated it.'

'Wow, that's weird,' Mrs Trifle said. 'I'd feel strange sailing in a ship that's been at the bottom of the sea.'

'Me, too,' Selby thought as a shiver shot up his spine. 'Sunken ships. Spooky-dooky.'

'There's nothing to worry about,' Gary told the Trifles. 'But seriously, people are begging to go on this cruise. Of course if they beg, they aren't allowed to go.'

'Why not?'

'Because beggars can't be *cruisers*. Woo woo woo,' Gary said, strutting around like a chicken as he did when he told a joke.

'Yes, very good,' Mrs Trifle said, still wondering about Gary's joke. 'But what will we do with Selby?'

'Bring him along. I'll tell the *Fun 'n' Happy Cruise* people that if they don't let Selby go, I won't go.'

'In that case,' Mrs Trifle said, 'count us in.'

'Oh boy, oh boy,' Selby thought. 'I'm going on a real live cruise. And I get to hear all of Gary's great jokes! This is going to be so much fun!'

Two days later, Selby and the Trifles boarded the *Rose Bouquet 2*.

'They haven't done a great fixing-up job,' Mrs Trifle said as she looked at the rust streaks down its sides.

'No,' Dr Trifle agreed. 'It looks like they've just spray-painted over the rust. Come on, let's find our stateroom.'

Down and down they went to the lowest deck. All along the walls Selby could see paint-covered bits of seaweed and barnacles.

'Sheeesh,' Selby thought. 'This ship gives me the heebie-jeebies. It reminds me of when I went down in that submarine and got stuck in the wreck of the *S. S. Humungous*. 🐾 I don't know if I'm going to like this.'

Soon the ship had cast off and Selby and the Trifles stood on the deck, watching the land disappear into the distance.

'Surely there wouldn't be any icebergs around here,' Mrs Trifle said, nervously, looking up ahead of the ship.

'It's possible,' Dr Trifle said. 'In fact the iceberg this ship hit when it was the *Rose Bouquet 1* was right near here. It must have drifted all the way up from the Antarctic.'

'I wish Dr Trifle hadn't said that,' Selby thought. 'Now I'm really nervous. Bad enough that this ship has already sunk once. Double sheeesh!'

🐾 *Paw note: If you want to read about that adventure see 'Selby Submerged' in the book* Selby Surfs.

S

'Captains don't always see icebergs,' Dr Trifle went on, 'because they're mostly under water with just a tiny bit sticking up. When they do see them it's often too late. Then the ice rips the ship apart.'

'Rips the ship apart, triple sheeeeesh!' Selby thought.

'I wish you hadn't told me that,' Mrs Trifle said. 'I'll have iceberg nightmares.'

'Me, too,' Selby thought. 'Now I've got icebergs on the brain.'

Suddenly there was the crackle of a loudspeaker.

'Hiya hiya hiya,' came Gary's voice. 'This is Gary Gaggs, your non-stop comic. I was just in the kitchen and this guy comes in with a fish in a fish tank. He says, "Do you know how to make fishcakes?" The cook says, "Certainly, sir." So the guy says, "Then make him a chocolate cake. It's his birthday." Woo woo woo.'

'I'm not sure I get that one,' Mrs Trifle said to Dr Trifle.

'Seriously, folks, the fish was swimming around in the tank with a cigarette in its mouth. It must have been a *puffer* fish. Woo woo woo.

There were these two fish in a tank. One of them says, "You drive and I'll shoot the gun." Get it? Two fish in a *tank*?'

'Hey, I like that one,' Selby thought.

'This pirate wanted to have his ears pierced,' Gary said. 'He had to pay a buccaneer. That's a *buck an ear*, folks. No kidding. There's this guy who orders three dozen oysters. His wife says, "Can I have one?" And he says, "No, get your own." She says, "That's very *shellfish* of you." Woo woo woo. Once I opened a hundred oysters,' Gary went on, 'then I pulled a mussel.'

'He pulled a mussel,' Selby thought. 'He's too funny! Oh, no! He's going to make me laugh!'

'I got seasick at lunchtime. I ended up having two lunches — one down and one up. Woo woo woo. Seriously, folks, my watch must have been very hungry — it went back for seconds. Get it? It went back *four seconds*. Oh, you're a lively group today. If you can't laugh, just throw money. I asked the waiter what was taking the cook so long and he said, "He's making spaghetti." I said, "But spaghetti isn't even on the menu." And he said, "He makes it just to *pasta* time." I think I'll give that guy a *pizza* my mind. Woo woo woo.'

'Oh, Gary,' Selby thought. 'You're brilliant!'

'Let's go up to the bridge,' Dr Trifle said.

'Bridge?' Mrs Trifle said. 'What bridge?'

'The bridge is a room where the captain steers the ship,' Dr Trifle explained. 'They said we can go up there at any time.'

Selby followed Dr and Mrs Trifle up to the bridge. There was an old man standing at the wheel.

'Captain Whitecap, at the helm,' he said. 'Welcome aboard.'

'Captain Whitecap?' Mrs Trifle said. 'Are you any relation to the Captain Whitecap who was the captain of the *Rose Bouquet 1*?'

'Yes ... I mean no ... I mean yes,' the man said. 'I mean it was me.'

'So you're the one who hit it?'

'Hit it?'

'The iceberg.'

'Please,' the captain said, clutching his chest. 'Don't use that word. It brings back terrible memories.'

'I'm sorry,' Mrs Trifle said. 'I was just surprised that you were the captain when this ship hit an ice … thingy and now you're the captain again.'

'Okay, so I made a silly little mistake once — twice — but that's all behind me now.'

'Twice?' Mrs Trifle said. 'You made *two* silly little mistakes?'

'Yes, I was the captain of the *S. S. Humungous* when it sank after it hit … when it hit an … an …'

'Did the *Humungous* also hit an … one of those things?' Mrs Trifle asked.

'It's so easy to do,' the captain sighed. 'There's only a bit of them sticking out of the water, you know. It didn't show up on the radar. By the time I saw it, it was too late. Have you ever tried to stop a ship like this? Or just turn it? It takes ages!'

Selby watched as a thick blanket of fog came towards the ship.

'Fog,' the captain said. 'I hate fog almost as much as I hate … you-know-whats.'

The captain hit the radar screen with his hand. The green screen flickered on and then went off again.

'Hasn't worked properly since we sank,' the captain said. 'I can't wait for this cruise to end. This'll be my last. Overdue to retire.'

'I think we'd better leave you to it,' Dr Trifle said nervously, opening the door.

'Leave your dog here to keep me company,' the captain said. 'Dogs are good luck on ships. Actually, it's cats that are good luck but he'll do. What's his name?'

'Selby,' Mrs Trifle said. 'We'll come back for him later.'

'This guy is so jumpy,' Selby thought after the Trifles had left the bridge. 'I think he should have retired years ago.'

Gary's voice came over the loudspeaker again.

'Hello again, folks,' he said. 'It's Gary Gaggs, your gaggy gag man again. Did you see that tiny island we passed a little while ago? It was just sand with one palm tree. There was a guy wearing nothing but rags. He was jumping up and down waving. I said to the captain, I said, "Who's that guy and what's he doing?" And the captain said, "I don't know. He does that every year when we pass by." Woo woo woo. Just kidding. This is a great ship, the *Rust Bucket*,'

Gary said. 'I mean the *Rose Bouquet*. Of course it's a bit of a sick ship. Do you know what a sick ship is? It's a boat that needs to see a *dock*.'

The captain let out a little laugh.

'Hey, this guy is good, isn't he, Selby?' he said.

'But seriously, folks. They would have scraped all the rust off this ship but they realised that the rust was the only thing holding it together. Woo woo woo.'

'That's so true!' the captain laughed. 'Why am I laughing?'

'What do you get when you cross an ocean with the *Rose Bouquet*? I'll tell you: *halfway*. See? It hit an iceberg. Ha ha ha ha. I love that one.'

'Iceberg?' the captain mumbled. 'Did he say *iceberg*?'

'But seriously, folks, this ship has lots of modern facilities,' Gary went on. 'You'll be able to have swimming lessons in your own cabins — after we hit another iceberg! Woo woo woo.'

'Ice . . . Ice . . .' the captain said.

'Oh, Gary,' Selby thought. 'No more iceberg jokes, please. You're freaking the captain out.'

'I've got lots more jokes,' Gary said. 'This is

just the tip of the iceberg. Woo woo woo. Why am I getting a sinking feeling? Woo woo woo.'

'Tip of the iceberg,' the captain mumbled. 'Sinking. Got to get out of here.'

'The captain is terrified,' Selby thought. 'He's not doing anything. He's just standing there.'

Selby put his paws up to the window and stood there, straining to see through the mist.

'Seriously, folks, the *Titanic* hits an iceberg, right?' Gary went on, 'And it's got a hole in the bottom. So the captain comes running up to this big guy. He says, "You're just the right size. Go down below, find the hole and push yourself down into it, legs first." And the guy says, "Will that keep us from sinking?" and the captain says, "No, but we're short one lifejacket." Woo woo woo.'

Suddenly Selby saw something white in the water up ahead.

'What is it? Is it the tip of an iceberg? The captain hasn't seen it. He's just frozen there! I've got to do something!'

Selby barked his loudest bark but the captain only turned around and sat down in a chair, muttering, 'Abandon ship. Abandon ship.'

'What am I going to do now?' Selby thought, whacking the radar screen on the side. 'Hey! It's coming back. The green line is going around and around. Oh, no! I think I see a blip straight ahead of us! There's something out there!'

Selby turned the wheel hard to the side but the ship kept going straight ahead.

'How do you drive this thing?' he thought. And then he said, out loud, 'Captain Whitecap! Do something! We're going to hit an iceberg!'

'Iceberg? . . . Iceberg?' the captain mumbled.

'The guy is completely out of it,' Selby thought, grabbing the microphone. Selby cleared his throat and put on his best captain's voice. 'This is your captain speaking. Go to the nearest lifeboats and get ready to abandon ship.'

Suddenly there was a burst of laughter from all around the ship.

'They think I'm Gary Gaggs!' Selby squealed in his brain. 'They don't believe me!'

'Seriously, folks!' Selby yelled and before he could say anything else there was another roar of laughter and people yelling, 'Woo woo woo.'

'Why did I say that?' Selby asked himself.

'No kidding...' he started but again there was laughter.

'What am I going to do? Hey! Everyone! There's an iceberg up ahead and we're about to crash into it!'

Suddenly there was silence. Then someone yelled, 'What's the punchline?'

'Hey! That doesn't sound like Gary Gaggs!' someone else yelled. 'It's not Gary!'

'It can't be,' the first someone yelled. 'Gary's already sitting in a lifeboat. Everybody to the lifeboats!'

Selby could see people running around the decks and lifeboats being lowered.

'Thank goodness,' he thought. 'Now it's my turn. Hey, Captain Whitecap! Snap out of it! Get a grip! Abandon ship! Oh, no! He's just sitting there! What can I do?'

Selby slapped the man in the face a couple of times. Then he heard the door behind him open.

'Selby!' Mrs Trifle yelled. 'Come quickly!'

'Here, boy,' Dr Trifle called.

Selby bounded out the door but Dr and Mrs Trifle suddenly stopped.

'Hey, the captain's still in here!' Mrs Trifle said, grabbing the man's hand. 'Come with us. It's okay. Everyone's ready to abandon ship.'

Before Selby knew it, they were sitting in a lifeboat, watching as the *Rose Bouquet 2* sailed on into the mist. And as the mist gradually cleared, Selby spotted the white thing again in the water.

'What is that?' Mrs Trifle asked. 'An iceberg?'

'I don't think so,' Dr Trifle said. 'It's much too small.'

'It's one of those plastic things to keep food cold,' Mrs Trifle said. 'Someone must have lost it off their boat.'

'Oh, no,' Selby groaned. 'I thought it was the tip of an iceberg. What have I done? We'll never catch up with the ship now and they'll blame poor old Captain Whitecap for this. I can't let it happen. I've got to tell everyone that it's my fault. My secret will be out but at least I won't feel bad about it for the rest of my life.'

Selby cleared his throat and put his paw up on the side of the lifeboat. He opened his mouth and —

'Get a look at this!' someone cried.

Suddenly there was a huge *creeeeeeekkkk!* and a *crooooorrrrrkkk!* and a *crash!* When the mist cleared there was the *Rose Bouquet 2* sinking nose down into the depths. Next to it was a huge iceberg.

'An iceberg!' everyone gasped. 'It's a good thing we all got off okay.'

'Three cheers for the captain!' someone yelled. 'If it wasn't for him we'd be at the bottom of the ocean by now!'

Everyone cheered.

Suddenly Gary said, 'Where's Mandy?'

'Mandy who?' Mrs Trifle asked.

'Mandy lifeboats, the ship just sank!' Gary laughed. 'Woo woo woo. Get it? I've got a million of them. But seriously, folks, this rich lady wants to send a letter so she goes to the post office and they sell her a stamp. So she says, "Do you mean I have to stick this on myself?" and the guy says, "No, stick it on the letter, you ninny." Woo woo woo.'

'That Gary is a joke genius,' Selby thought as he struggled not to laugh. 'His ship can sink but he'll never lose his old magic.'

# ANIMAL ANGELS

'I love this show,' Selby thought. 'It's the best thing on TV. If I ever get really sick I'd love to have an Animal Angel look after me.'

Selby had just watched the latest episode of *Animal Angels.* In it veterinarians race around the world helping to rescue animals that are sick or injured. In this program there had been a kitten in France that couldn't sleep, a dog in Brazil that wouldn't eat, and a little bird with a broken beak clinging to a cliff in China.

'That was soooooo sad when they had to put that poor little birdie down,' Selby thought as he blinked back a tear, 'but they'd tried everything to fix him up and nothing worked. Anyway, I

17

loved it when the vets operated on the kitty's crook neck so that she could sleep again. But that dog with *Gutsitis Scrambulitis* — now that was amazing!'

The dog had been born with a very rare condition. His insides were all in the wrong places. At first the vets didn't know what was the matter. The main thing was that he'd lost his appetite. Then they noticed that his stomach was sore. After that he threw up, his tongue became dry, and his back legs shook. The vets worked out the problem and operated just in the nick of time.

'Those guys are so clever!' Selby thought. 'But what a gory operation. They cut his whole belly open from top to bottom and then shifted everything back to where it was supposed to be. If I'd have watched it properly I wouldn't have been able to eat for a week. But speaking of eating . . .'

Selby trotted into the kitchen and looked in his bowl.

'Dry-Mouth Dog Biscuits,' he thought. 'When are the Trifles going to realise that I hate them? Hey, hang on, it was Mrs Trifle's birthday yesterday. Dr Trifle got takeaway food from The Spicy Onion Restaurant. I'll bet there are some leftovers.'

Selby gobbled six peanut prawns, three big spoonfuls of potato salad and a huge slice of meat. After that he ate all the bits of mango in the fruit salad and he was just starting into a huge slice of chocolate birthday cake when Aunt Jetty's dreadful sons Willy and Billy burst through the door.

'Hey, Unkie!' Willy screeched. 'Look at the dog! He's in the fridge! See?'

Selby crammed the cake into his mouth and shut the fridge door just as Dr Trifle came into the kitchen.

'I'm sorry, what did you say?' he asked.

'That poopy doggy was in the fridge!' Billy yelled.

'In the fridge?' Dr Trifle said, as he put the big jar of Snap-Bond Ultra Glue he'd just bought on the kitchen bench. 'Don't be silly, boys. Selby is a dog. He doesn't get into fridges. He wouldn't even fit.'

'No no no, Unkie!' Willy cried. 'He opened the door!'

'Are you telling a fib again, Willy?' Dr Trifle asked.

'No, no, and he can talk and everything! Cross my heart!' 🐾

'Boys, listen to me. I've got important work to do in my workroom. You watch TV or something. Mrs Trifle will be here soon,' Dr Trifle said, heading off down the hallway. 'And don't you dare be mean to Selby, do you hear?'

'Yes, Unkie,' the boys said.

'Hey, Billy,' Willy said. 'Remember that TV show? Remember about cutting up that stupid doggy?'

'Yeah. That was so good,' Billy said.

'Hey, listen, Billy.'

Willy whispered in his brother's ear.

'If Willy is thinking what I think he's thinking then I'm going to bite him into next week,' Selby said to himself. 'I'm getting out of here!'

'Unkie!' Willy called. 'Selby's sick!'

🐾 *Paw note: Why, oh why, did I ever let Willy know my secret? (See 'Wild West Willy Rides Again' in the book Selby's Secret.)*

S

20

'No, I'm not. What's he on about?' Selby thought.

Dr Trifle opened the door to his workroom.

'What do you mean?' he asked.

'He didn't eat nothing,' Willy said.

'Yeah, his doggy bowl is full,' Billy said.

'Hmmm, that is strange,' Dr Trifle said, having a closer look. 'We filled it up this morning but he hasn't eaten anything.'

'And I couldn't eat another thing after all that birthday cake,' Selby thought.

'He was chucking,' Billy said.

'I *what*? What's this kid on about?' Selby thought.

'What do you mean, chucking?' Dr Trifle asked.

'Frowing up like this,' Billy said, pretending to throw up. 'Nuffing came out but.'

Dr Trifle bent down and touched Selby's head.

'He seems okay to me,' Dr Trifle said. 'Now I've really got to get some work done, kids. Please don't disturb me.'

'Thank goodness he doesn't believe them,' Selby thought as Dr Trifle went back to his workroom. 'But I'd better eat something to show I'm not sick.'

Selby forced himself to eat the whole bowl of dog biscuits as Willy and Billy watched cartoons on TV. Then Billy turned around and looked into the kitchen.

'Hey, Willy!' he said. 'That poop-face ate his dinner.'

'No, he didn't.'

'Yes, he did!'

'No, he didn't,' Willy said, filling Selby's bowl again with Dry-Mouth Dog Biscuits. 'See? It's full.'

The boys laughed and then went back to watching TV.

'I'll show those brats,' Selby thought as he struggled through another bowlful. 'I'd throw it in the garbage but the Trifles might find it.'

But once again, the boys filled Selby's bowl and once again Selby ate all the dog biscuits.

'Hey, Billy!' Willy said, grabbing Dr Trifle's Snap-Bond Ultra Glue. 'I've got an idea.'

Willy filled the bowl again with dog biscuits and then mixed in some glue and stirred them around. In a second, they were glued solid.

'Unkie!' Willy called. 'Hey, Unkie!'

'I'll teach them,' Selby thought as he licked furiously at the biscuits. 'If I keep this up long enough, the biscuits will dissolve. Oh, woe, they're killing my tongue!'

Just then Mrs Trifle came home.

'Auntie!' Willy said. 'Selby's sick and frowing up and everything!'

'I'm sick of these stupid biscuits,' Selby thought.

'Is he really?' Mrs Trifle asked, kneeling down next to Selby. 'Hmmm. He's off his food. I've never known him to just lick at it like that. He hasn't eaten since last night.'

'Uh-oh,' Selby thought, as Mrs Trifle pressed harder on his stomach. 'If she keeps touching me she's going to make me throw up.'

'Goodness,' Mrs Trifle said, as Selby pulled away from her. 'His stomach must be sore.'

'Yes, and his legs were shaking, like this,' Willy said, making his own knees wobble back and forth.

Willy pointed to Selby's hind legs just as Selby finally gave up the struggle and threw up all over the kitchen floor.

'Oh, you poor darling,' Mrs Trifle said. 'Not eating. Sore stomach. Throwing up. Back legs shaking. I wonder what could be wrong?'

'They're lying!' Selby thought. 'Oh, please Mrs Trifle, don't believe them.'

'It's just like on *Animal Angels*!' Billy squealed. 'Call them, Auntie!'

'*Animal Angels*?' Mrs Trifle said. 'Oh, yes, I know that program. Maybe they'll know what's wrong.'

Mrs Trifle grabbed the telephone and rang the *Animal Angels*' number and told them about Selby.

'Whatever you do, don't move him,' the woman on the phone said. 'The van just happens to be in your area. We'll be right over.'

Minutes later a huge van screeched to a stop outside the Trifles' house and two vets jumped out and ran to the door. Dr and Mrs Trifle were waiting for them.

'From what you said on the phone, Mrs Trifle,' one vet said, 'your dog has a very rare disease called *Gutsitis Scrambulitis*.'

'Guts what?'

'Scrambled guts. He was born with his

innards out of order,' the other vet explained. 'His heart is where his liver should be and his kidneys are where his lungs should be.'

'Is this serious?' Dr Trifle asked.

'Is this *serious*? Did you see our last TV show?'

'No, I'm afraid I didn't.'

'Well, let's put it this way. If we don't open him up and unscramble him right now, then he's history. Do we have your permission?'

'No,' Selby thought.

'Yes,' Mrs Trifle said. 'Whatever you can do to save Selby, please do it.'

'Look, he's trembling all over and there's sweat pouring off him,' one of the vets said. 'That's Stage Two.'

'Stage Two?'

'That's what happens next after loss of appetite, dry tongue and rubbery legs. He's definitely internally scrambled.'

'Of course I'm trembling and sweating, you ninny,' Selby thought. 'You would be too if you were about to be operated on and you were perfectly okay.'

'Quick, get him into the van. We have our mobile operating theatre in there,' the other vet said. 'Let's open him up before he gets to Stage Three.'

'Stage Three?' Dr Trifle said.

'Scraping sounds in the back of the throat. Wiggly jaw,' the vet said. 'If he gets to that point then his chance of survival is very slim. Let's go.'

Selby could see Willy and Billy giggling as the vets carried Selby to the van.

'This is it,' Selby whimpered in his brain. 'I've got to talk! I've got to tell them that those lying little brats made everything up! I'm not having those *Animal Angel* vets cut me open and unscramble my guts when they aren't even scrambled in the first place!'

The van doors were folded back. Inside was an operating table and rows and rows of shiny operating instruments. One of the vets turned on some bright lights.

'But what if I talk and give away my secret and then something happens? What if Willy and Billy feel guilty and confess before they cut me open? Things like that are always happening to me at the last possible second, just when I'm about to give away my secret. It's happened

tonnes of times. I can't talk just yet! — I can't! I've got to wait till the last tiny fraction of a second.'

Selby watched as they strapped him to the table and got their instruments ready. The vets put on masks and gowns and funny little cloth booties over their shoes.

'I've got to hold out!' Selby thought. 'I know something's going to happen and everything's going to be okay.'

Dr and Mrs Trifle and Willy and Billy peered in from outside the van.

'Poor Dr and Mrs Trifle,' Selby thought. 'They're as scared as I am. Well, maybe not quite ...'

Selby looked over at the beaming faces of Willy and Billy.

'Those little mongrels,' Selby thought. 'Some day I'm going to get them. Boy, am I going to get them!'

One of the vets picked up a knife thingy.

'This is it,' Selby thought. 'It's talking time. Better not wait another teeny tiny fraction of a second.'

Selby cleared his throat and was about to say,

'Excuse me, but don't believe a word that Willy and Billy have said. I'm not sick and don't you dare cut me open!' when one of the vets looked at him in horror.

'That's it! He's definitely got it! Listen to the scraping sounds in his throat! He's wiggling his jaw! Quick! Put him to sleep!'

Selby yelled out, 'Hang on a tick!' But he was too late. The other vet had clamped one of those clear plastic putting-you-to-sleep-before-an-operation thingies over his mouth and the next thing Selby knew he was drifting into a deep sleep and thinking of the dog on TV and the gory operation that was too horrible to watch.

'Too late…' Selby thought, as everything went dark. 'I'll get those brats … I'll bite … them … till … they . . . . . . . . . . . . . . scr … ea … mmmmmm …'

Soon there was music in Selby's ears. Beautiful music that drifted through the air — music that he was sure he'd heard before.

Then slowly Selby opened his eyes. The vets and the Trifles were bending over him.

'That was a close call,' one of the vets said.

'I'll say,' the other vet said. 'If you hadn't noticed that the dog biscuits were all glued together, Dr Trifle, things could have been very serious.'

'They didn't operate?' Selby thought. 'Do I dare look at my tummy tum tum? No! They didn't!'

'Poor darling Selby,' Mrs Trifle said, holding him in her arms. 'It's a good thing you didn't know what was about to happen to you. And as for you, boys,' she said, turning to her nephews, 'I don't believe in spanking children, but in your case I'm afraid I had to make an exception.'

Selby looked over at the boys, who were wiping the tears from their eyes.

'So that was the heavenly music I heard — the wonderful sounds of Willy and Billy bawling their eyes out. Oh joy! Oh double joy!'

# SELBY ON GLASS

It was the wee hours of the morning in the big city. The sun was still a pink glow below the horizon. Everyone was asleep, everyone except Dr Trifle, Mrs Trifle and Selby. It was an ordinary morning but for one thing — Selby was walking on glass.

Not broken glass in the street.

Not a piece of glass lying on the footpath.

No, Selby was walking up the outside of the newly built skyscraper, the Crystal Tower, his paws clinging magically to the glass sides. Dr and Mrs Trifle were holding a safety net below.

'This is *sooooo* scary,' Selby thought. 'But it's great, too!'

Selby lifted one paw at a time, placing each one carefully against the glass before lifting the next.

'These things are amazing!' he said, looking at his special gloves and socks. 'I'm not slipping a bit.'

'Selby,' Dr Trifle called from the footpath below. 'Come down, boy, before someone sees you.'

Selby looked up at the building towering above.

'Don't make me come down yet,' he thought. 'Just let me go a tiny bit higher.'

'Selby, come here,' Dr Trifle called again.

'Psssst! Selby!' Mrs Trifle said, clapping her hands. 'Here, boy!'

'I'll pretend I can't hear them,' Selby thought. 'Oh, this is so much fun!'

Selby scrambled up and down the glass, moving this way and that, while Dr and Mrs Trifle called and called to him.

After a while Selby thought, 'I guess I'd better do as they say.'

But just as he thought this, he noticed something.

What he noticed were cars racing down the street and people running from all directions. Soon there were five police cars, three firetrucks, an ambulance, and two TV news crews stopped out the front.

'Gulp,' Selby gulped. 'They're going to find out about Dr Trifle's secret invention and it's all my fault! I should have gone down when they told me to. Oh, woe woe woe ...'

We'd better start this story the day before in the Trifles' house in Bogusville.

It was then that Dr Trifle came out of his workroom, smiling from ear to ear. He was holding something behind his back.

'Flies have amazing feet when you think about it,' he announced.

'I don't think about flies' feet very often,' Mrs Trifle said, looking up from her newspaper.

'You mean you've never wondered how they can walk up walls?'

'Not really. They must have sticky gooey stuff on their feet.'

'No, no. Sticky gooey stuff would just collect dirt and lose its stickiness. Then they'd slide down and fall on the floor — only they wouldn't really because they can fly.'

'I guess that's why they call them *flies*,' Mrs Trifle said. 'Do they have suction cups on their feet?'

'Suction cups are too much work,' Dr Trifle said. 'The flies would have to keep pulling them loose and then pushing them back on. They'd be exhausted in no time. No, they have teeny weeny itty bitty hairs on their feet.'

'How do little hairy feet let them walk up walls?'

'I have no idea,' Dr Trifle said, 'but it works.'

'My sister, Jetty, has hairy feet,' Mrs Trifle said, 'but she can't walk up walls.'

'Just as well,' Dr Trifle said. 'She tracked mud around the floor last time she was here. It's a good thing she wasn't walking on the walls as well.'

'There's a very strange woman they call the Human Fly,' Mrs Trifle said. 'She climbs up cliffs, skyscrapers, lighthouses. You name it, she climbs it. She doesn't get permission or anything. She just sneaks up things and lets them arrest her when she gets to the top. Now I remember. Her name's Clemenza Lightfoot.'

At the mention of the Human Fly's name, Selby's ears shot up.

'Clemenza Lightfoot,' he thought. 'She's *sooooooo* amazing! Just thinking about her makes my little heart go pitter pat. I just love the way she yells, "Hi-ho! and up I go! So long, suckers!" I reckon she's the bravest person in the world.'

'Of course she doesn't climb the way a fly does,' Dr Trifle said. 'She uses ropes and bits of metal. Now if she had my Wall Walkers she wouldn't need anything else.'

With this Dr Trifle took a pair of socks and gloves from behind his back. He put them on and tightened the straps around his wrists and ankles. Then, with one great leap, he threw himself against the wall.

'Goodness gracious!' Mrs Trifle cried. 'You're stuck to the wall. How will I ever get you off?'

'I'm not stuck,' Dr Trifle said. 'I can move. Watch.'

Mrs Trifle and Selby watched as Dr Trifle put one hand up and then a foot up and slowly walked up the wall.

'That's fantastic!' Mrs Trifle cried.

'I thought of them when I fell off that ladder last month,' Dr Trifle said. 'With these Wall Walkers there's no more need for ladders. Just put them on and off you go — like a real fly.'

'But how did you invent them? You said that you didn't even know how flies' feet work.'

'Simple. These *are* flies' feet. Look,' Dr Trifle said, pulling a glove away from the wall and showing it to Mrs Trifle. 'Remember all the dead flies we vacuumed out of the attic last winter?'

'I certainly do,' Mrs Trifle said, moving closer. 'I filled three vacuum-cleaner bags with them.'

'Well, I saved them and then glued their little feet to these gloves and socks. So now I have flies' feet — thousands and thousands of them.'

'Oh, yuck!' Mrs Trifle exclaimed. 'That's disgusting.'

'The only disgusting thing is that my ankle is still so sore from falling off that ladder that I can't climb properly.'

'Aren't you afraid that those old dried flies' feet will break off and you'll come crashing down?'

'No. There are thousands and thousands of them. If enough of them broke off I'd slide slowly down, that's all,' Dr Trifle said, stepping down from the wall. 'Here, you have a go.'

'No way! Keep those filthy things away from me!'

'Then I'll have to get someone else to give them a proper test.'

'Me me me!' Selby thought.

'Now who could we get?' Dr Trifle said, slowly turning towards Selby.

Before Selby knew it the socks and gloves were being tightened around his paws. Then Dr Trifle picked him up, put his feet against the wall and slowly let go of him.

'I'm standing on a wall!' Selby thought. 'I can't believe this!'

'Look, he's walking!' Mrs Trifle said. 'He's going right up the wall!'

'He's walking across the ceiling,' Dr Trifle cried. 'He's Selby, the human fly — I mean Selby, the *dog* fly!'

'This is *sooooo* much fun!' Selby thought as he walked around in circles over the Trifles. 'I feel as free as a bird!'

'People will be able to climb anything with these,' Dr Trifle said. 'Utility poles, trees, buildings. Window-washers can use them on tall buildings instead of those things they have to stand in.'

'Surely they won't work on glass,' Mrs Trifle said.

'Why not? 🐾 flies walk on windows all the time. I know, let's give them the ultimate glass test. Let's see if they work on the brand new office building in the city, the Crystal Tower.'

'Oh boy, oh boy, oh boy,' Selby thought. 'I'm going to love this!'

And so it was that Selby found himself part way up the Crystal Tower bright and early the next morning. And that's where Selby was when he noticed the commotion in the street below.

'Oh, phew!' he said as he stood perfectly still so no one would notice him, 'they're all running around the corner. Something else is happening here. I'd better get down before someone sees me.'

🐾 Paw note: This is my specially invented question-comma. You can use it in the middle of sentences. Good, hey?

S

Suddenly a woman's voice yelled, 'Hi-ho! and up I go!' and then she added, 'So long, suckers!'

'It's her!' Selby squealed. 'It's Clemenza Lightfoot, the Human Fly! The bravest person in the world! She's making a sneak attack on the Crystal Tower!'

Selby scurried across to the side of the building and then peeked around the edge. There, on the other side, was Clemenza, smacking the suction cups on her hands and feet against the glass with a *Psssht*! and then pulling them loose with a *Tha-kunk*! as she made her way up the building.

'Come down, Ms Lightfoot!' a police officer yelled. 'You're under arrest!'

'I'll see you at the top, cop!' Clemenza yelled back. 'And good luck getting there because the lifts aren't working yet. Yahoo!'

*Tha-kunk*! *Psssht*!

Selby crept up and up, peering carefully around the side of the building as the woman made her way higher.

*Tha-kunk*! *Psssht*! *Tha-kunk*! *Psssht*!

'Look at the muscles,' he thought. 'Wow! What a woman!'

Clemenza was halfway up the tower when she stopped to catch her breath. Sweat was pouring off her.

'Dr Trifle was right about those suction thingies being hard work,' Selby thought. 'But you can do it, Clem!'

Suddenly a low cloud came in, covering the tower in mist.

'This is spooky,' Selby thought. 'I can't see the street or the top of the tower anymore. And I can barely see Clemenza.'

Clemenza was mumbling under her breath.

'I'm so exhausted,' she said. 'I don't know if I can do this . . . I'm so out of breath . . .'

'Keep going, Clem!' Selby muttered.

'. . . I . . . I've got to do it . . . Can't go down . . . too high up.'

Selby watched as Clemenza started up again.

*Tha-kunk! Psssht! Tha-kunk! Psssht! Tha-kunk! Psssht! Tha-kunk! Psssht! Tha-kunk! Psssht! Tha-kunk! Psssht! Tha-kunk! Psssht! Tha-kunk! Psssht! Tha-kunk! Psssht! Tha-kunk! Psssht! Tha-kunk! Psssht! Tha-kunk! Psssht! Tha-kunk! Psssht! Tha-kunk! Psssht! Tha-kunk! Psssht! Tha-kunk! Psssht! Tha-*

*kunk! Pssssht! Tha-kunk! Pssssht! Tha-kunk!*
*Pssssht! Tha-kunk! Pssssht! Tha-kunk! Pssssht! Tha-*
*kunk! Pssssht! Tha-kunk! Pssssht! Tha-kunk!*
*Pssssht! Tha-kunk! Pssssht! Tha-kunk! Pssssht! Tha-*
*kunk! Pssssht! Tha-kunk! Pssssht! Tha-kunk!*
*Pssssht! Tha-kunk! Pssssht! Tha-kunk! Pssssht! Tha-*
*kunk! Pssssht! Tha-kunk! Pssssht! Tha-kunk!*
*Pssssht! Tha-kunk! Pssssht! Tha-kunk! Pssssht! Tha-*
*kunk! Pssssht! Tha-kunk! Pssssht! Tha-kunk!*
*Pssssht! Tha-kunk! Pssssht! Tha-kunk! Pssssht! Tha-*
*kunk! Pssssht! Tha-kunk! Pssssht! Tha-kunk!*
*Pssssht! Tha-kunk! Pssssht! Tha-kunk! Pssssht! Tha-*
*kunk! Pssssht! Tha-kunk! Pssssht! Tha-kunk!*
*Pssssht! Tha-kunk! Pssssht! Tha-kunk! Pssssht! Tha-*
*kunk! Pssssht! Tha-kunk! Pssssht! Tha-kunk!*
*Pssssht! Tha-kunk! Pssssht! Tha-kunk! Pssssht! Tha-*
*kunk! Pssssht! Tha-kunk! Pssssht! Tha-kunk!*
*Pssssht! Tha-kunk! Pssssht! Tha-kunk! Pssssht! Tha-*
*kunk! Pssssht! Tha-kunk! Pssssht! Tha-kunk!*
*Pssssht! Tha-kunk! Pssssht! Tha-kunk! Pssssht! Tha-*
*kunk! Pssssht! Tha-kunk! Pssssht! Tha-kunk!*
*Pssssht! Tha-kunk! Pssssht! Tha-kunk! Pssssht! Tha-*
*kunk! Pssssht! Tha-kunk! Pssssht! Tha-kunk!*

*Pssssht! Tha-kunk! Pssssht! Tha-kunk! Pssssht! Tha-kunk! Pssssht! Tha-kunk! Pssssht! Tha-kunk! Pssssht! Tha-kunk! Pssssht! Tha-kunk! Pssssht! Tha-kunk! Pssssht! Tha-kunk! Pssssht! Tha-kunk! Pssssht! Tha-kunk! Pssssht! Tha-kunk! Pssssht! Tha-kunk! Pssssht! Tha-kunk! Pssssht! Tha-kunk! Pssssht! Tha-kunk! Pssssht! Tha-kunk! Pssssht! Tha-kunk! Pssssht! Tha-kunk! Pssssht! Tha-kunk! Pssssht! Tha-kunk! Pssssht! Tha-kunk! Pssssht! Tha-kunk! Pssssht! Tha-kunk! Pssssht! Tha-kunk! Pssssht! Tha-kunk! Pssssht! Tha-kunk! Pssssht! Tha-kunk! Pssssht! Tha-kunk! Pssssht! Tha-kunk! Pssssht! Tha-kunk! Pssssht! Tha-kunk! Pssssht! Tha-kunk! Pssssht! Tha-kunk! Pssssht! Tha-kunk! Pssssht! Tha-kunk! Pssssht! Tha-kunk! Pssssht! Tha-kunk! Pssssht! Tha-kunk! Pssssht! Tha-kunk! Pssssht! Tha-kunk! Pssssht! Tha-kunk! Pssssht! Tha-kunk! Pssssht! Tha-kunk! Pssssht! Tha-kunk! Pssssht! Tha-kunk! Pssssht!*

'You can do it, Clem!' Selby muttered again. 'Just a little bit to go!'

*Tha-kunk!*

'What was that? Did someone say something?' Clemenza said.

'Ooops,' Selby thought, ducking around the corner. 'I think she saw me.'

*Pssssht! Tha-kunk! Psssht! Tha-kunk! Psssht!*

Selby pulled himself tight against the glass and kept perfectly still. A head peered around the corner. The head was connected to the body of the bravest person in the world, Clemenza Lightfoot. Its eyes opened wide and then its mouth opened wider.

'*Yiiiiikkkkkeeeeesss!*' it screamed. 'A dog! I'm terrified of dogs!'

Suddenly Clemenza Lightfoot went limp.

'Oh, no! She's fainted!' Selby thought. 'I can't believe she's scared of dogs! I'd better get out of here before she comes to.'

Selby started down.

*Tha-kunk!*

'What was that? Oh, no, one of her hand suction cups has come loose! If I don't wake her up, they'll all come loose!'

Selby scrambled closer. He grabbed the woman's hand and pressed it against the glass.

*Psssht!*

'Wake up!' he cried. 'You're losing your suction!'

*Tha-kunk!*

'Oh no, the other hand's come loose!'

Selby reached out with his paw and pressed Clemenza's other hand against the glass.

*Psssht!*

But, no sooner had he done this than, *Tha-kunk!* A foot came loose.

Selby pushed Clemenza's foot against the glass.

*Psssht!*

And then, *Tha-kunk!* Another hand came loose.

'Clem! Wake up!'

*Psssht!*

'I can't keep this up forever!' Selby took one of his gloves off the glass and slapped the Human Fly's face once — and then again.

'Wake up!' he cried, whacking her with the other glove, and suddenly noticing the flurry of flies' feet falling towards the ground.

'Ooops,' he said, 'they're breaking off. I'd better go easy.'

'What?... What?...' Clemenza mumbled. 'What's breaking off? Oh no, another dog!'

'I'm not a dog!' Selby said. 'Calm down. Would I be talking if I was a dog?'

'No, you've got a point,' the woman said. 'Then what are you?'

*Tha-kunk!*

'I'm a person in a dog suit,' Selby said. 'But never mind about that, your foot just came loose! Push it back again, quick!'

'Oh, okay.'

*Pssssht!*

'So what are you doing up here? Are you trying to beat me to the top or something?'

*Tha-kunk!*

'No, I'm not! But never mind about that, Clem, your left hand just came loose again!'

*Psssht!*

'That's better,' Selby said, 'now start climbing! You're almost there!'

'I can't,' the woman sighed. 'I'm too exhausted.'

'If you don't, you'll fall!' Selby said. 'Come on, Clem, right hand ...'

*Tha-kunk! Psssht!*

'Now left foot ...'

*Tha-kunk! Psssht!*

'Atta girl, Clem ...'

*Psssht! Tha-kunk! Psssht! Tha-kunk! Psssht! Tha-kunk!*

Little by little Selby and Clemenza Lightfoot moved towards the top of the building.

'I can't do it,' Clemenza gasped. 'I can't.'

'You have to! You're almost there! One more step!'

*Tha-kunk! Psssht!*

Clemenza grabbed the railing at the top of the tower and pulled herself up and over. Then she turned and leaned down, putting out her hand.

'Grab my hand, little guy,' she said.

Selby stretched out a paw but suddenly sensed himself slowly slipping.

'Oh, no! I'm sliding!' Selby screamed. 'Save me!'

But it was too late, Selby's front paws had lost their grip and he spun around, pointing downward. His back paws held him for a second but then he started sliding faster and faster down the side of the building.

'I'm going down!' he cried.

'No, no, don't go!' Clemenza yelled after him. 'I want to know who you are!'

Like a skier going full speed down a ski slope, Selby slid through the mist towards the ground. Before he knew it he was lying on the footpath staring up at the startled Dr and Mrs Trifle.

'Oh, Selby,' Mrs Trifle said, picking him up in her arms. 'Thank goodness, you're safe!'

'Good boy,' Dr Trifle said, taking the Wall Walkers off Selby's paws and throwing them in a rubbish bin. 'I guess these were a bit of a dud. It's a pity because they seemed to work brilliantly at first. Oh, well.'

That night back in Bogusville, the Trifles watched the evening news. They saw Clemenza Lightfoot being taken away in a police car.

'What is she raving about?' Dr Trifle asked. 'Something about a man in a dog suit talking to her and helping her get to the top.'

'I told you the woman was a bit strange,' Mrs Trifle said.

Suddenly Dr and Mrs Trifle turned towards Selby.

'A man in a dog suit?' Mrs Trifle said. 'You don't suppose ... ?'

'But there's no way Selby could have *talked* to her,' Dr Trifle said.

'Still,' Mrs Trifle answered, 'I think something strange happened up there on that building today. It was a pity we couldn't see because of the mist.'

'You mean we *missed* something because of the *mist*,' Dr Trifle laughed.

'I guess you could say,' Selby thought, 'that it will always be a mist-ery.'

# SELBY SPORTS STAR

'Soccer?' Dr Trifle said. 'I have no idea how to play soccer. Is it a card game? Or is it that game where you throw rubber chickens into a bathtub?'

'Neither, silly,' Mrs Trifle said. 'There's a ball and you kick it up and down the field till someone gets a goal.'

'What's a goal?'

'That's when someone kicks the ball into this sort of a box thingy. Only there's a goalie trying to keep it from going in.'

'I don't understand this sports business,' Dr Trifle said. 'In every sort of game there's someone trying to do something and someone else trying to stop them. Why don't they just take turns? That way everyone will get lots of points and they'll all stay friends and no one will get hurt.'

'Poor Dr Trifle,' Selby thought. 'He has no idea. He's the least sporty person in the whole world.'

'But it wouldn't be any fun,' Mrs Trifle said. 'Now I hope you don't mind but you and I are going to be playing soccer for Bogusville against Poshfield. Don't worry, I'll tell you what to do. It's just a friendly match.'

'Friendly? Against Poshfield? Are you sure? It seems to me that things can be quite *un*friendly if Poshfield's mayor, Denis Dorset, has anything to do with it. Is he going to play?'

'No.'

'Good.'

'He'll be the referee,' Mrs Trifle said. 'And don't worry, he can't cheat because I have a copy of the rules right here,' Mrs Trifle said, holding up a book called *Soccer for Ninnies*. 'I've been studying them for weeks.'

'If I'm going to play this soccer thing I'd better get into shape,' Dr Trifle said. 'I think I'll start by walking around the house once a day and then I'll do some thumb flexes and some bending over.'

'There's no time for that. The game starts in fifteen minutes,' Mrs Trifle said, handing her husband a pair of shorts and an *I Luv Bogusville* T-shirt. 'Get into these. Oh, and Selby can be our mascot and bring us good luck.'

'Oh, boy!' Selby thought. 'I love soccer! I watch it all the time on TV when the Trifles are out. I can't wait to see Bogusville thrash those poncy Poshfield guys.'

At the soccer field Denis Dorset was wearing a striped referee's uniform and a whistle hung around his neck.

'Let's see who's playing for Bogusville,' Selby thought. 'There's Melanie Mildew, she could be okay; Camilla Bonzer, I'm not so sure about her; Postie Paterson, good; and Aunt Jetty is the goalie. They used to call her Shin-Smasher Jetty when she played hockey. I reckon she'll be a really good goalie. Oh, and there's Gary Gaggs, he could be okay. Not a great team but the Poshfield team looks pathetic. Look at them in their neat little uniforms. They look like they've just come from the hairdressers and had their fingernails polished. And that's just the guys. I reckon they'll be in for a big surprise.'

'It's about time you got here,' Denis Dorset said to the Trifles. 'Now are you ready to play?'

'Well, yes, I think so,' Mrs Trifle said.

'Then how about a little wager?'

'A what?'

'A bet. I'll bet you ten thousand dollars that we'll beat you.'

'Ten thousand dollars!' Mrs Trifle said. 'We don't have that sort of money. Besides, I'm not really a betting person.'

'Then we'll make it one thousand. Just take it out of the tea money jar in your council's recreation room. That's what we did.'

'Our council doesn't even have a recreation room and our tea money jar never has any more than seventy cents in it.'

'Oh be a sport, Mayor Trifle,' Denis said, rubbing his hands together. 'Or are you afraid we'll beat you?'

'Not at all. I think we should just play for the fun of it.'

'Fun? You're such a bunch of scaredy-cats.'

'No, we're not.'

'If these Poshfield twits really want to lose their money,' Aunt Jetty roared, 'let's take it from them! What do you say? Let's all chip in and take the bet! Come on, guys!'

'I'll be in that!' Melanie Mildew yelled.

'Me too!' said Postie Paterson.

'And me!' Gary Gaggs said.

One by one, the Bogusville players called out.

'Okay, Denis,' Mrs Trifle said, 'a thousand dollars it is.'

A cheer went up from the Bogusville players as the two mayors shook hands.

'Great!' Selby thought. 'This is just *tooooooo* good!'

Denis Dorset blew his whistle.

'Okay, the game has officially started,' he said. 'But wait. I do believe you're one player short, Mayor Trifle. I'm afraid you'll have to forfeit the game.'

'I beg your pardon?'

'Your team just lost. I'm terribly sorry but those are the rules,' Denis said, holding up his copy of *Soccer for Ninnies*. 'You only have ten players and you need eleven. Sorry. We'll take the thousand dollars in cash, thank you very much.'

The Poshfield team all laughed and began putting on their designer tracksuits.

'That is so not fair!' Mrs Trifle said. 'You knew we only had ten players before you made the bet. That's cheating!'

'It's not cheating,' Denis said. 'It's just noticing. It's a pity you didn't notice, too. You could have saved your players a considerable amount of money.'

Mrs Trifle thumbed through her copy of *Soccer for Ninnies*.

'Hang on,' she said. 'Selby is our eleventh player.'

'Selby?' Denis Dorset asked. 'Who's that?'

'Our mascot,' Mrs Trifle said, pointing to Selby. 'And now he's going to be a player, too.'

'You can't have a dog on your team!'

'Show me where it says that the players have to be human beings.'

'Of course it's not in the rule book,' Denis said. 'It's too obvious. Everyone knows that already.'

'We don't know that, do we, team?' Mrs Trifle called.

'No, we don't!' came the reply.

'There you have it then,' Mrs Trifle said.

'I'm sorry but our team refuses to play against a dog,' Denis said. 'He might bite.'

'He most certainly will not!' Mrs Trifle answered. 'But if you're worried about it we'll just let him sit and watch the game. And, by the way, I've been noticing something myself: Poshfield is short a player. That'll be a thousand dollars, please.'

'You tell him, Mrs Trifle,' Selby thought. 'That dirty guy! He's getting everything he deserves.'

Denis smiled.

'No, we do have another player. He's getting dressed. Carlos! Are you ready?'

A man ran onto the field. Denis threw him the ball and he caught it on his toe and kicked it up over his head and when it came down he kicked it back over again with his heel. For a minute, everyone just stood and stared as the man kept the ball in the air with his feet, his knees and his forehead.

'Wow!' Selby gasped in his brain. 'Where did this guy come from?! He's fantastic! Carlos? Carlos who? I'm sure I've seen him before. Hang on a tick, Carlos Rodrigues! He's the guy who scored the winning goal in the World Cup Final last year. In fact, he scored *all* of the goals in the World Cup Final.'

'That's Carlos Rodrigues!' Camilla Bonzer said and gasped (out loud). 'He scored all of the goals in the World Cup Final!'

'He can't play for you,' Mrs Trifle said. 'This is a game between Poshfield and Bogusville. He doesn't live in Poshfield.'

'For the moment, he does,' Denis said.

'But he's a professional. Professionals aren't allowed to play against amateurs.'

'What's the difference between an amateur and a professional?' Denis asked.

'Professionals play for money.'

'Then we're all professionals,' Denis said. 'Because we're playing for a thousand dollars.'

'That is sneaky and mean,' Mrs Trifle said. 'Denis Dorset, you tricked us!'

'Me? My dear lady, I did nothing of the kind. Now can we please get this game started?

Or would you just like to hand over the money and save yourself a lot of embarrassment?'

'We'll play!' Aunt Jetty shouted. 'Won't we, guys?'

There was a moment of silence and then a mumbled chorus of, 'I guess so's', and 'Okay, all right's', and 'If you say so's'.

Mrs Trifle turned to Selby.

'Stay here, boy,' she said.

'Oh, how I'd love to play,' Selby thought. 'I wish I could kick a soccer ball.'

Then the game started and Carlos dribbled the ball up the field towards the goal and Aunt Jetty. Bogusville players raced in from all directions but Carlos kicked the ball between their legs, or chipped it over their heads, or even bounced it off them only to get control of it again.

'This isn't fair!' Selby squealed in his brain. 'None of them has a hope of even touching the ball. Look! They're falling all over the place!'

Soon Carlos was facing Aunt Jetty.

'Atta boy, Carlos!' Denis yelled. 'Shoot! Shoot!'

But Carlos just smiled and turned around,

dribbling the ball back in the other direction, weaving around the Bogusville and Poshfield players.

'What are you doing?' Denis shouted. 'The goal is that way! What are we paying you for?'

'You pay me to play,' Carlos said. 'I play. I have good time.'

'Well, you'd better win the game,' Denis said.

Suddenly Carlos kicked the ball hard, straight up in the air. And as it came down, he did a bicycle kick up and over his head, shooting the ball straight back towards Aunt Jetty.

There was terror in Aunt Jetty's eyes as the ball tore towards the goal, making a high-pitched whistling noise as it flew through the air. Aunt Jetty dived to the side to get out of the way, only to have it accidentally hit her arm and bounce out. Jetty jumped to her feet and grabbed the ball in her hands.

'I'll show you, you boofhead!' she screamed, throwing it down the field.

Carlos stopped and wagged his finger at Aunt Jetty.

'Is not nice, Crazy Lady,' he said. 'You make Carlos sad you say thees thing.'

And off he went again, tearing towards Aunt Jetty. This time she stood with her legs apart and her arms out, ready to block any attempt at goal. But Carlos stopped and stood with his foot on top of the ball.

'Go ahead, you nong!' Jetty yelled. 'Don't just stand there!'

This time Carlos stepped back and kicked the ball very gently up and into the corner of the goal. Aunt Jetty jumped for it but she didn't have a chance of stopping it.

'One to nothing — Poshfield!' Denis yelled. 'Good one, Carlos!'

'Thank you, Boss.'

Moments later Carlos was kicking the ball up and down the field again.

'See,' he said, 'now I do square pass — to me. And I do reverse pass — to me. I chip zee ball ... up up up and look! He come down to me again.'

'This is terrible!' Selby sighed. 'Nobody but Carlos has even touched that ball. He just kicks it back and forth and does whatever he wants. We don't have a hope!'

When the whistle blew for half-time, the

Bogusville players stumbled off the field, exhausted, while the Poshfield players — who had spent their time standing around doing nothing — pranced off to open their picnic hampers.

'Poor Dr Trifle,' Selby thought, 'he's hardly moved but he's still exhausted.'

When the second half started, Carlos again had total control of the ball.

'Now watch, Mister Boss,' he said, winking at Denis.

Suddenly, Carlos kicked the ball fast along the ground, making it bounce off Gary Gaggs' feet and then off Dr Trifle's feet and then off Mrs Trifle's feet before they knew what was happening. Then, after bouncing off Camilla's feet it went straight into the Bogusville goal.

'One all!' Mrs Trifle yelled.

'Carlos!' Denis screamed. 'What did you do that for?'

'I make game interesting,' Carlos said. 'Now is big fun.'

'Well you'd better make it big win, Carlos, or you won't get paid!'

'Mister Boss worry too much.'

Once again the ball went back and forth and up and down but always in Carlos's control.

'This is awful!' Selby wailed in his brain. 'This is a disaster!'

'Thirty seconds to go!' Denis Dorset yelled. 'Come on! Finish them off!'

'Okay, Boss.'

Carlos gathered speed, racing around the Bogusville players and came face to face with Aunt Jetty. He let a long, curving shot rip towards the goalie. Aunt Jetty jumped to the side, the ball catching her on the head and sending her crashing to the ground.

'She's lying there gasping for breath!' Selby thought. 'She can't get up! Denis should be blowing his whistle and stopping the game! But he's not! That dirty guy! And look, the ball bounced back to Carlos. He's about to shoot again! This is so unfair! I can't let this happen.'

Like a shot out of a cannon, Selby tore onto the field, moving so fast that Carlos, who was just drawing his foot back, didn't even see him go past. Once again the ball whistled by at the speed of a bullet. But by the time it got to the goal, Selby was standing on his hind legs on top of the gasping lump that was Aunt Jetty.

'I've got to stop this even if it kills me!' he thought. 'I can't let it go in! If I can stop it, it'll be a tie and the Bogusville team won't lose their money!'

What happened next is unclear. Selby later remembered jumping into the path of the ball, hitting it with his head and sending it back onto the field again.

But it was the last thing he remembered. He woke up hours later lying on the Trifles' carpet. Mrs Trifle was holding an icepack to his forehead.

'He's coming round,' Mrs Trifle said. 'I think he's going to be okay. Oh, you beautiful dog, you,' she said, cuddling him.

Dr Trifle stood there smiling and shaking his head.

'You certainly saved the day, Selby,' he said. 'And it's a good thing you were a player on the team and not just a mascot or it wouldn't have counted.'

'Yes,' Mrs Trifle said, 'I don't suppose he knew what he was doing. Dogs just seem to have this instinct to chase sticks and balls and things. Poor little guy,' she added. 'That ball really hit him hard, poor darling.'

'I feel a bit sorry for Carlos,' Dr Trifle said.

'He's such a good player — and to lose to us! Goodness me.'

'Well, if you ask me, he was too good for his own good,' Mrs Trifle said. 'If he hadn't kicked the ball as hard as he did Selby would have just knocked it out of the goal. But no, it bounced all the way down to the other end and into the Bogusville goal.'

'It did?' Selby thought. 'You mean I actually scored a goal? I beat the best soccer player in the whole world?! It can't be!'

'That Denis Dorset is not a happy man,' Dr Trifle said with a laugh. 'Did you see the look on his face when he had to pay you the money?'

'I certainly did,' Mrs Trifle said. 'Good old Selby. Didn't I tell you he'd bring us luck?'

'You certainly did,' Dr Trifle said. 'You know I think I like this soccer business after all. We were really getting into it towards the end, don't you think?'

Selby struggled not to smile as he looked up at Dr and Mrs Trifle.

'They may not be very sporty,' he thought, 'but I love them all the same.'

# SELBY IN THE SLAMMER

'Your dog is under arrest,' announced Denis Dorset, the mayor of Poshfield.

'Under arrest?' Mrs Trifle exclaimed. 'You can't arrest Selby because you lost the soccer game.'

'Nothing to do with that. You are obviously unaware of Poshfield's new leash law. No dog is allowed to walk around without a leash.'

The mayor of Poshfield stood smirking on the doorstep. Behind him were six police officers. And in front of him, held firmly by his leash, was Powderpuff, the mayor's vicious poodle.

'Mr Mayor,' Mrs Trifle said, 'you are in

Bogusville, not Poshfield. We don't have a leash law in Bogusville.'

'You tell that idiot,' Selby thought.

'This may be Bogusville,' Denis said, 'but your dog was in Poshfield without a leash.'

'Was I?' Selby thought.

'Was he?' Mrs Trifle asked.

'He was seen running through our beautiful town with no leash and no one to control him. That may be good enough for Bogusville but it's not good enough for us. Poshfield people are nice people and we like everything to be nice. Out-of-control dogs are definitely not nice.'

'But how would Selby have got to Poshfield?'

'On the fifteenth of last month he was running riot through our fair town,' Denis Dorset said, grinning a thin grin. 'We have a photograph to prove it.'

Powderpuff strained on his leash, baring his teeth at Selby and growling.

'Now I remember,' Selby thought. 'I was out for a walk and minding my own business when old fang-face here chased me into Poshfield.'

'Show me the photograph,' Mrs Trifle demanded.

'It's in here,' Denis said, holding up a laptop computer. 'You will see it in court.'

'This is absurd! You can't put a dog on trial.'

'Wrong, Mayor Trifle. We can and we will.'

'But how can a dog defend himself?'

'You may defend him if you wish,' Denis said.

'I don't care about your silly law!' Mrs Trifle said. 'Selby's staying right here. Go away!'

Denis turned to his police officers.

'Cuff him,' he ordered.

Before Selby could think to blink, he was grabbed, paw-cuffed and bundled into a police paddy wagon. Within ten minutes, he was in a crowded courtroom.

'This is like a nightmare,' he thought. 'I can't believe it's happening!'

The judge rapped his hammer on the desk just as Dr and Mrs Trifle dashed into the courtroom.

'Thank goodness the Trifles are here,' Selby thought.

'Don't worry, Selby,' Mrs Trifle whispered. 'We'll get you out of this.'

'Poshfield Court will come to order,' the judge said. 'Selby Trifle, you are charged with being without a leash. Do you have anything to say for yourself?'

'Now hold the show!' Selby thought (he didn't say it, he only thought it). 'Of course there's something I have to say for myself: I was chased here. It wasn't my fault!'

'Would someone like to speak for the dog?' the judge said.

'Yes, Your Honour,' Mrs Trifle said. 'I don't believe that Selby was ever in Poshfield — at least not since the leash law was passed.'

'Wrong,' Denis Dorset said, calmly turning on his laptop.

Suddenly a photo appeared on a big screen at the front of the court. It clearly showed Selby running down the main street of Poshfield.

'Here is the proof,' Denis Dorset said. 'See the date code on the photo? That's one month after our wonderful leash law was passed. Look at that monster's face. Look at the hatred in his eyes, the bare teeth ready to tear the flesh of some innocent Poshfield person.'

'I was scared, that's all!' Selby thought. 'Old shark-mouth was right behind me nipping at my tail! You just can't see him because he's not in the photo.'

'I'm stunned,' Mrs Trifle said.

'Maybe he's not the sweet and innocent pet you think he is,' the judge said.

'That's it,' Selby thought. 'I'm gone. Dr and Mrs Trifle will have to pay a fine. But if I tell them the truth I'll give away my secret. It's not fair to the Trifles but it's better if they pay the fine. I'll make it up to them somehow.'

'I find Selby, the dog, guilty,' the judge said, rapping his hammer again.

'Okay,' Dr Trifle sighed. 'What's the fine?'

'According to this new law there is either a ten thousand dollar fine or ten years in prison.'

'Prison? For a dog?' Mrs Trifle exclaimed. 'Is this a joke?'

'This is not a joke, Mayor Trifle. And the one who decides which it will be is Mayor Dorset. I am sorry but I don't make the laws. The Poshfield Council does that.'

'But-but-but you can't put a dog in prison!' Dr Trifle cried.

'Oh yes, I can,' Denis Dorset said, rubbing his hands together. 'And I will — unless you do us a favour.'

'And what might that be?'

'Give the town of Bogusville to Poshfield.'

'Why, you sneak! You passed that law and you caught Selby just so that you could take over our town, didn't you?' Mrs Trifle said in a very cranky voice.

'Come, come, Mrs Trifle, you're just angry because you didn't think of it first. Bogusville is a perfect place for us to dump our rubbish. Our sewers will empty into Bogusville Creek and we'll send our poor people — not that we have many — to live in Bogusville. Poshfield will be the nicest town in Australia and, perhaps, the world.'

'Hey, that dirty guy!' Selby thought. 'He can't get away with this!'

'That's outrageous!' Mrs Trifle yelled. 'The people of Bogusville would never let you turn our town into your rubbish tip and sewer!'

'Is that your final answer?' Denis asked.

'It certainly is!'

'My advice to you, Mrs Trifle, is to convince your council to go along with the Poshfield Plan. If they don't agree, then it's bye-bye to your dog for a long, long time. I'll give you till tomorrow to decide.'

The judge rapped his hammer again.

'Take the dog to prison,' he said. 'Bring him back tomorrow for sentencing.'

Selby lay on a bed in his cell at Poshfield Prison.

Across from him was a big man covered in tattoos and snoring loudly.

'What's to become of me?' Selby whimpered.

As he looked up through the bars on the window to the stars above tears rolled down his cheeks.

'It'll be ten years till I see the Trifles again,' Selby mumbled. 'I'll never see their kind and loving faces again, except when they come to visit — *if* they come to visit. They must be so angry with me. I wish I could tell them what really happened.'

'Hey, you! Shut up!' the man said. 'I'm trying to get some sleep.'

'Oh, no!' Selby thought. 'He heard me!'

The man rolled over and looked at Selby.

'I'll just pretend I didn't say anything,' Selby thought. 'He'll think it came from the next cell.'

'Hey, dog,' the man said, 'what's your problem?'

Selby closed his eyes and lay perfectly still.

'Dog, I'm talking to you. What are you on about? You're not fooling me. I know you're awake.'

'What does it matter about my secret now?' Selby thought. And then he said out loud, 'Okay, okay. My problem is that I'm in prison.'

'Yeah, well that's my problem, too. So keep the noise down.'

The man rolled over again.

'This is amazing,' Selby thought. 'I just talked and he doesn't seem to care at all. Hey, you,' Selby said out loud again, 'didn't you notice that I talked?'

'So what? Go to sleep.'

'But I'm a dog. I'm not supposed to talk. I don't know how I learned to do it. It just happened. I was sitting in front of the TV one day and suddenly I could understand what they were saying.' 🐾

As Selby talked about his life with the Trifles, the man slowly sat up on his bed listening to every word. On and on Selby talked till the

---

🐾 *Paw note: To see exactly how this happened read the story 'Selby's Secret' in the book* Selby's Secret. **S** middle of the night. He talked about Dr Trifle's inventions, and about Mrs Trifle's troubles as mayor, about Willy and Billy — everything.

Finally, he had said it all.

'That's really interesting,' the man said. 'And trust me, I won't give away your secret.'

'You won't?'

'I would but nobody would believe me.'

'They wouldn't?'

'No, because I'm a liar. I've been a liar all my life. From when I was a little kid I never ever told the truth,' the man said. 'Hey, I like you, dog. What's your name?'

'Selby,' ❤ Selby said.

'Call me Tats,' the man said. 'So how long are you in for?'

'I'll find out tomorrow. Ten years, I think.'

'Wow! That's a long time in a dog's life. What was the evidence?'

'A photo of me running through Poshfield without a leash.'

The man gave a long, low whistle.

❤ Paw note: *I told him my real honest and true name but I can't tell you. (Sorry.)*

S

'It's hard to argue with a photograph,' he said. 'Did you realise you were set up?'

'What do you mean?'

'It wasn't a coincidence that the mayor's poodle chased you into Poshfield. This mayor guy would have been spying on you. Then one day you were out near Poshfield and he had his mutt chase you over the line. Was there a car behind you?'

'Come to think of it, I think there was.'

'That was the mayor. He let his dog out of the car and then took pictures when you got into Poshfield. That's what I reckon.'

'But that's *sooooooooo* unfair!' Selby wailed. 'I'm going to tell the judge everything.'

'It'll be your word against that mayor guy. And he's got a photo. Besides, if you talk, your life will be ruined forever. You said that yourself.'

'It's already ruined.'

'No, it isn't,' Tats said. 'How about escaping?'

'Escaping? Sure — but how?'

Tats grabbed one of the window bars. He slid it up easily and then took it out.

'Can you fit through there?'

'How'd you do that?' Selby asked.

'Years of work. Last week I finally got it loose. But now I don't need to escape because they're letting me out next month. Come on, off you go, little guy.'

Selby climbed up onto the windowsill.

'Thank you so much,' he said as he jumped down to the ground.

'Pssst!' Tats pssst-ed. 'Where will you go?'

'Home,' Selby whispered back.

'But you can't. Sooner or later the cops will get you. You can't go home ever again. Go as far away as possible. Someone will take you into their home.'

'But I don't want anyone else. I only want to live with the Trifles. They're the most wonderful people in the world.'

'Selby, take it from an old crim: you need a plan. Everyone needs a plan. Forget these owners of yours and work out a plan for the rest of your life. Now go!'

Selby dashed across the road and through the darkened streets of Poshfield.

'It's nice to be free,' he thought, 'but what good is freedom when I can't (*sniff*) live with the Trifles? And it's all because of that horrible

Denis Dorset and that bloodthirsty dog of his. If I ever see him again I'll bite him into next year!'

Suddenly Selby caught sight of Poshfield Manor, the mayor's mansion.

'Hey, hang on,' he thought. 'What was it Tats said? "It's hard to argue with a photograph."'

In a second, Selby was through the gate and peering through the windows of Denis Dorset's house. Soon he was looking into the mayor's study.

'The laptop!' he thought, as he quietly raised the window and climbed in. 'It's sitting right there. Oh boy, oh boy.'

Selby turned on the computer.

'And there's the photo.'

Selby was about to hit the DELETE button when he had a second thought.

'I'd better check to see if there are other copies saved somewhere.'

Selby clicked his way through the computer files, looking for copies of the photo until suddenly —

'Whoa!' he cried in his brain. 'He took stacks of photos! Me walking along. Me walking along some more. Powderpuff chasing me into Poshfield.'

Suddenly Selby heard the unmistakable sound of Powderpuff's claws clicking down the hall outside the study. In a second the dog was standing in the doorway, his fangs dripping with saliva.

'Hey, Powderpuff,' Selby whispered. 'Have you ever seen a dog disappear? Watch me!'

Selby dived out the window and was running again.

'That's two escapes in one night,' he thought. 'And now for one more. Only this'll be an in-scape instead of an e-scape.'

And it was a startled Tats who woke up the next morning and looked over at the other bed.

'Selby!' he said. 'You're back!'

'Yes, I'm back,' Selby said. 'And I have a plan.'

'This court is now in session,' the judge said, banging his hammer. 'Now to sentence Selby Trifle to prison.'

'One moment, please,' Mrs Trifle said. 'Could we see the evidence again?'

'I can't see that it will do any good,' the judge said, 'but all right.'

Denis Dorset again opened his laptop and showed the photo of Selby on the screen.

'I think that's proof enough,' he said. 'Now, Mrs Trifle, have you considered our little proposal? It's still possible to get your dog off.'

'I love Selby,' Mrs Trifle said. 'He's the most wonderful, kind and loving dog in the whole world and I will miss him. I'll visit him every day in prison and bring him lots of those Dry-Mouth Dog Biscuits that he loves so much. But I can't let Bogusville be ruined by you!'

'Poor Dr and Mrs Trifle,' Selby thought, his eyes filling with tears.

Suddenly Mrs Trifle reached over to Denis's laptop and clicked the mouse. The photo on the screen changed. There was Selby walking along. Another click and there was Powderpuff chasing Selby.

'What are you doing?' Denis yelled. 'Leave my computer alone!'

'Stay away from me, you ... you ... you worm!' Mrs Trifle yelled back.

There was a gasp in the courtroom as the photo came up of Selby being chased past the sign that said: ENTERING POSHFIELD.

'Denis Dorset, you are a sneak and a scoundrel!' Mrs Trifle cried. 'You planned all this just to get your grubby hands on Bogusville.'

'I-I-I don't know what you're talking about,' Denis Dorset said.

'Well I do,' the judge said. 'And it is clear that Selby is innocent ...'

The police undid Selby's paw-cuffs and Selby bounded across the courtroom and into the Trifles' arms.

'... and,' the judge continued, 'that you are guilty, Denis Dorset.'

'Of what, you silly man?' Denis said. 'There's no law against chasing dogs.'

'But there *is* a law against dogs being out without a leash in Poshfield. I believe you and your council wrote that law. And your dog Powderpuff was running down the street in Poshfield without a leash. Look at your own photos.'

'This isn't fair!'

'Oh, yes it is! Now which will it be: ten years in prison for the dog or a ten thousand dollar fine for you?'

'I'm thinking, I'm thinking,' Denis said, sheepishly. 'Oh well, I guess I'll pay the fine. I wouldn't feel right about little Powdie going to jail.'

'That was brilliant!' Dr Trifle said to Mrs Trifle when they got home. 'How did you know to click the mouse on the laptop?'

'I got an email last night telling me to do it,' Mrs Trifle said.

'So who sent the email?' Dr Trifle asked.

'I don't know. There was no name on it. The funny thing was that it had Denis's email address on it. He obviously didn't send it. I guess I'll just have to say that a little birdie told me.'

Dr and Mrs Trifle laughed. Selby looked up at them.

'But it wasn't a little birdie that told her,' Selby thought, 'it was a little doggy — little old me.'

# 'SELBY, TELL ME!'

It all began with an email. It was like so many emails that Selby had answered before. It said:

DEAR SELBY,
MY NAME IS FLEUR. I'LL BE TEN YEARS OLD
NEXT WEEK ON APRIL 1ST. APRIL FOOLS' DAY.
I JUST LOOOOOOOOOVE YOUR BOOKS! I'VE READ
EVERY SINGLE ONE EXCEPT MAYBE THREE OR FOUR
OF THEM. PLEASE, SELBY, TELL ME YOUR REAL
NAME. I PROMISE I WON'T TELL ANYONE —
EVER! CROSS MY HEART AND HOPE TO DIE,
STICK A NEEDLE IN MY EYE.
YOUR NUMBER ONE FAN,
FLEUR

*Paw note: You probably know that my real name isn't
Selby. My real name is a secret.*

S

83

'Hmmm,' Selby hmmmed. 'Why do kids always want to know my real name? I guess they're just curious.'

HIYA FLEUR,
THANX FOR YOUR EMAIL. HAPPY BIRTHDAY FOR NEXT WEEK! I HOPE YOU GET LOTS OF GREAT PRESSIES. I'M SO GLAD THAT YOU LIKE MY BOOKS. I'M REALLY SORRY BUT I CAN'T TELL YOU MY REAL NAME. I NEVER TELL *ANYONE* SO DON'T TAKE IT PERSONALLY.
CYA,
SELBY

DEAREST SELBY,
PRETTY PLEASE WITH SUGAR ON TOP TELL ME YOUR REAL NAME. I JUST HAVE TO KNOW. I WON'T READ YOUR BOOKS ANYMORE IF YOU DON'T TELL ME.
YOUR BESTEST FRIEND,
FLEURINA

HIYA FLEURINA,
YOU WON'T READ MY BOOKS ANYMORE? NOW YOU'VE HURT MY FEELINGS.
CYA,
SELBY

Dearest sweetest Selby the most wonderful dog in the world,
I'm so sorry. I was just kidding. I will always read you books even when I'm too old for them. Honestly you are my very fave dog in the universe and I just have to know your real name. I promise, promise, promise I won't tell even if they hold me down and tickle me to death.
ILYH (I Love You Heaps),
Fleur

Hiya Fleur,
Sorry but the answer is still nope.
Cya,
Selby

Dearest wonderful Selby,
Why not? It's only little me and I won't tell a single-bingle soul.
Your Best Friend,
Honest Fleur
XOXOXOXOXOXOXOXOXOXOXO

Hiya Honest Fleur,
Here's my problem: If I tell anyone my real name then they might tell someone else. And that someone else will tell

SOMEONE ELSE. SOONER OR LATER SOMEONE WILL
SAY, 'HEY, THERE'S A DOG WITH THAT NAME
LIVING IN MY TOWN'. BEFORE I KNOW IT
THERE WILL BE HUGE CROWDS OUTSIDE MY HOUSE
TAKING PICTURES OF ME AND TRYING TO GET ME
TO TALK. MY LIFE WOULD BE RUINED!
BESIDES, THE TRIFLES MIGHT MAKE ME WORK
AROUND THE HOUSE. I DON'T WANT TO BE
THEIR SERVANT. I JUST WANT TO BE THEIR
PET.
CYA,
SELBY


DEAR SELBY,
DON'T WORRY! I ABSOtiveLY POSIluteLY
WON'T TELL ANYONE!!!!!!!!!!!!!!
DON'T YOU TRUST ME? DO YOU THINK I'M NOT
JUST A LITTLE GIRL BUT REALLY SOME SORT OF
RICH AND POWERFUL EVIL GENIUS WHO LIVES IN
THE TALLEST BUILDING IN THE BIGGEST CITY
IN THE WORLD AND OWNS LOTS OF TV STATIONS
AND WILL FIND YOU AND MAKE YOU TALK ON TV
AND MAKE HEAPS AND HEAPS MORE MONEY? IS
THAT WHAT YOU THINK? HOW COULD YOU
POSSIBLY THINK THAT?
LOVE FROM THE GORGEOUS, WONDERFUL,
BRILLIANT, AND TALENTED
FLEURINA, THE GIRL WHO IS GOING PLACES
(BUT NOT TO BOGUSVILLE SO DON'T WORRY.)

Selby paced around the Trifles' study.

'I don't want to hurt her feelings,' he thought. 'She sounds like a nice kid. How can I make her understand that if I tell anyone my real name I'll never feel safe again? That every time a car door opens in the middle of the night I'll wake up in a panic? That I'll never be able to go out without looking at people and wondering if they're about to dognap me?'

HIYA FLEURINA,

OF COURSE I TRUST YOU AND OF COURSE I DON'T THINK YOU'RE AN EVIL GENIUS WHO OWNS TV STATIONS AND WANTS TO MAKE HEAPS MORE MONEY BY TELLING THE WORLD MY SECRET. BUT WHAT IF I TOLD YOU MY NAME AND OKAY YOU DIDN'T MEAN TO TELL ANYONE BUT YOU TALKED IN YOUR SLEEP AND SOMEONE HEARD YOU? THEN MY SECRET WOULD BE OUT. SO PLEASE DON'T ASK ME AGAIN BECAUSE I REALLY AND TRULY CAN'T TELL YOU. AND THAT'S FINAL.

CYA,

SELBY

'There are times when I just have to be firm,' Selby thought. 'Oh, no, she's written back already.'

DEAR HANDSOME, BEAUTIFUL (IN CASE YOU'RE
REALLY A GIRL-DOG AND YOU'RE JUST FIBBING
ABOUT BEING A BOY-DOG) SELBY,
I DON'T TALK IN MY SLEEP, I PROMISE. I
KNOW BECAUSE MUM SAYS I DON'T. AND I'M
REALLY REALLY GOOD AT KEEPING SECRETS LIKE
TWO YEARS AGO I BROKE THE BIG FRONT
WINDOW IN OUR HOUSE AND I NEVER TOLD MUM
AND DAD I DID IT. BUT IT'S OKAY IF YOU
DON'T TELL ME. I UNDERSTAND. I GUESS I
WOULDN'T TELL ME EITHER IF I WAS YOU.
ANYWAY, I'M FEELING REALLY REALLY SAD
BECAUSE GREENIE, MY BUDGIE, DIED LAST
WEEKEND. AND NOW BLUEY, MY OTHER BUDGIE,
IS ALL ALONE. GREENIE USED TO PECK AT HIM
ALL THE TIME BUT I THINK HE LIKED IT.
JUST WATCHING BLUEY NOW MAKES ME CRY AND
CRY AND CRY BECAUSE HE'S SO SO LONELY.
YOUR VERY VERY TERRIBLY SAD AND UPSET NO.
1 BEST FRIEND IN THE WHOLE WIDE WORLD.
LOVE,
FLEUR

'Poor Fleur,' Selby thought. 'It's tragic when a
pet dies. I wish I could cheer her up. Maybe I
should tell her my name after all. What harm
could it do? Hmmm, I'd better think about it.

I think it's time for a good long thinking-walk.'

Selby turned off the computer and started walking. He walked and he walked and he walked and as he walked, he talked and talked to himself.

It went something like this:

'Okay, let's just say that I tell Fleur my name and she tells her parents.

*Hey, Mum, Dad, guess what? Selby is a real dog! I emailed him and he told me his real name!*

Her mother would say, *Don't be silly. He's a made-up dog. There's no such thing as a talking dog.*

*But, Mum, there is! Selby rings up Duncan Ball and tells him his stories. Duncan writes them down. The books are true!*

*If you say so, dear.*

*He lives in a country town here in Australia. Now that I know his name we could find him.*

*Do you know how many towns there are in Australia? There must be thousands of them. Even if he really did exist and you did know his name it could take years to find him.*

*We could pay a private detective. Selby's real name is kinda weird. A detective could find him, I'm sure.*

*Do you know how much private detectives charge, Fleur?* her dad would say. *And it could take months, or even years. Then what if this Selby doesn't really exist?*

*Oh, I guess you're right. Maybe we shouldn't look for him.*

'No grown-up is going to believe a kid when she says that I'm a real talking dog,' Selby thought. 'Even her friends won't believe her.'

Selby turned and started for home. He chuckled to himself as he thought of the evil genius who Fleur had made up, the one who owned lots of TV stations. Selby pictured an old man sitting at a huge desk, running his bony fingers through his long, grey hair and staring at his computer. He pictured the man cackling as he pretended to be a little girl in order to get Selby to tell him his real name.

'I love kids,' Selby thought. 'They have such great imaginations.'

That night when the Trifles were sound asleep, Selby sneaked into the study and turned

on the computer once again. And this is what
he wrote:

> HIYA FLEUR,
> I'M SO SORRY THAT GREENIE DIED. MAYBE
> YOU COULD ASK FOR ANOTHER BUDGIE FOR YOUR
> BIRTHDAY. NOW LISTEN, I'VE DECIDED TO
> TELL YOU MY REAL NAME. ARE YOU READY FOR
> THIS? MY REAL NAME IS ACTUALLY SELBY. 🐾
> BUT REMEMBER, YOU'RE NOT ALLOWED TO TELL.
> ANYONE. EVER. NO. MATTER. WHAT.
> CYA,
> SELBY

'Phew!' Selby phewed. 'I feel good now. I hope
that cheers her up. And it was really so easy.'

> DEAREST DARLING SELBY,
> OH, YOU DEAR DEAR WONDERFUL DOG, YOU!
> THANK YOU! THANK YOU! THANK
> YOU!!!!!!!!!!!!! YOU ARE SUCH A
> FANTASTIC DOG! I LOVE YOU TO DEATH! MY
> LIPS ARE SEALED. MMMMMMMMMMMMM.
> LOVE AND HUGS AND KISSES,
> FLEUR, THE TIGHT-LIPPED TERROR

🐾 *Paw note: Sorry, I can't tell you what I told her.*      S

91

Meanwhile, somewhere at the top of the tallest building in the biggest city in the world an evil genius sat behind his enormous desk. He stared at a computer screen and he cackled as he ran his bony fingers through his long, grey hair.

'Sucked in!' he cried. 'Dead budgie. Sad little Fleur. What a mug that mutt is. I practically told him who sad little "Fleur" really was — me! I even mentioned April Fools' Day, for pity's sake. Now who's the April fool? You stupid dog! I'll teach you to match wits with a rich and powerful genius.'

The old man pushed a button on his desk and a beautiful young woman appeared in the doorway.

'You seem very happy, sir,' she said.

'Yes, Olivia, I've just got myself a dog.'

'But you hate dogs, sir.'

'This is no ordinary dog. This is the most *extraordinary* dog in the world. And he is about to make me very very rich.'

'But you're already very very rich, sir.'

'True, but I am only the *second* richest person in the world. This dog is about to make me the *richest*. Get me a team of private detectives —

get a hundred of them. Make that a thousand. See if the police will get involved. There's no time to waste. We're going on a dog hunt.'

'Do you mean you don't know where this new dog of yours is?'

'I know that he lives in a country town somewhere in Australia. His name is Selby 🐾 — a very unusual name. We'll soon find him and get him to talk. And when he talks, everyone in the world will be watching him on my TV stations.'

'This dog talks?'

'Oh, yes,' the old man said. 'He certainly does.'

A few days later Mrs Trifle came home late from work after a long meeting.

'Have you heard the news?' Dr Trifle said. 'Something very exciting is happening!'

'What is it?'

'Do you know the dog in those books? Selby, the talking dog?'

🐾 *Paw note: I can't let Duncan write down my real name, so I'll just keep it as Selby. Sorry.*   S

'Yes, of course. Everyone knows Selby. I've often thought that he was a bit like our Selby — only our Selby can't talk. Why?'

'Well, it turns out that he's real. He is an actual real live talking dog.'

'Noooooooo!' Mrs Trifle exclaimed. 'How can a dog talk?'

'Apparently it's true. There's this live TV show and they reckon they've found him. They're about to catch him and get him to talk. Quick! It's on TV right now. Everyone in the whole world is watching.'

Dr and Mrs Trifle dashed to the TV and watched a team of detectives quietly surround a house under the cover of darkness.

'That's him now,' one of the detectives whispered. 'He's been out for a walk and he's coming home. Get ready to grab him.'

'But, hang on, isn't that the mayor's dog?'

'Don't worry about the mayor. We're working for Mr Big, and Mr Big doesn't worry about little mayors of dinky little Australian towns.'

'But what if the dog won't talk?'

'After a few days under a spotlight and not

being able to sleep, he'll talk. And if that doesn't work, we'll hypnotise him. Don't you worry, one way or another that mongrel will spill the beans.'

Dr and Mrs Trifle watched as the dog walked towards the house. Suddenly floodlights lit up the front yard.

'Get him, guys!' a detective yelled, throwing a net over the unsuspecting dog.

'Goodness me,' Dr Trifle said. 'Now wait just a minute! Isn't that Denis Dorset's dog, Powderpuff?'

'It certainly is,' Selby thought as he lay beside the Trifles, watching the scene on TV and trying not to smile.

'It certainly is,' Mrs Trifle said. 'Honestly, I hate this sort of program. Now I suppose they'll take Powderpuff away and try to get him to talk and that'll be on TV, too. I can't say that I'm especially fond of the dog but I do feel just a wee bit sorry for him.'

'I wonder where they got the idea that Powderpuff was a talking dog?' Dr Trifle asked. 'Surely a real talking dog would be smarter than him.'

'I not only would be,' Selby thought, 'I am. And if there's a lesson in this it's that you can never be too careful about telling people your secrets.'

# MILD-MANNERED MILES

'Excuse me, Madam, I'm terribly sorry to intrude but my name is Miles and I'm here to help you.'

The man at the door wore a grey suit and a thin black tie. His shoes were shiny and his hair was parted in the middle. In his hand he held a black briefcase.

'This guy has to be the most boring person I've ever seen,' Selby thought. 'Even the way he talks puts me to sleep.'

'What sort of help?' Mrs Trifle asked.

'With your accounts and bookkeeping. Bills to be paid. Cheques to be written. Books to be kept. Adding. Subtracting. Taxes. Bank balances. Keeping track of your money. I'm a door-to-door bookkeeper and accountant.'

'I've never heard of a door-to-door bookkeeper and accountant,' Mrs Trifle said.

'I may be the only one. I just happened to be passing by and I could see that your dining-room table and floor is covered in folders and papers. That is a sure sign of someone in financial difficulty.'

'Yes, and I'm at my wits' end,' Mrs Trifle sighed. 'I'm so confused. The situation is hopeless.'

'Nothing is ever hopeless, Madam,' the man said. 'Allow me to help you.'

'It's not me who needs help,' Mrs Trifle explained. 'It's the council. But I'm the mayor and I also look after money matters. I've been so busy that I've got behind. Now I don't know who's paid their rates and who hasn't. The electricity people are about to shut off the lights. And the council workers haven't been paid for weeks.'

'Why not start by paying them?' the man said.

'Because I can't find the council's cheque book. Oh, Mr Miles, I feel like I'm suffocating in paperwork!'

'It's Miles Manerd,' the man said. 'But call me Miles. And don't worry about a thing, dear lady. When can I start?'

'But I don't even know if the council has enough money to pay you.'

'Let me sort out the accounts,' the man said. 'If there isn't enough money in the bank then it'll be bad luck for me. If there is then I'll only charge my usual modest fee.'

'But there's days and days of work here,' Mrs Trifle said. 'Do you live nearby?'

'No, I live in the city.'

'Where will you stay? How will you pay for your meals?'

'How would it be if I stayed here with you and your husband?'

'Oh, Miles!' Mrs Trifle exclaimed, throwing her arms around the man. 'You're a lifesaver!'

'Please, please,' the man said, turning a deep shade of red. 'I'm only an accountant.'

Miles got to work straightaway. He started by putting all the folders in piles in the study and then vacuuming the study floor. When he finished he started vacuuming the rest of the house.

'I'll do that when I get back from the council. Dr Trifle would do it but he's very busy with a new invention,' Mrs Trifle said. 'Cleaning surely isn't part of your job?'

'Oh, but it is,' the man said. 'I can't work until I've made everything clean and tidy, spick and span. Clean house, clear mind, that's what I always say. You go to work. I'll have this finished very soon and get to work on the accounts.'

Selby watched as Miles cleaned the study floor and then cleaned all the other floors in the house. When he was finished he washed the dishes, mopped the kitchen floor, cleaned all the windows, polished the furniture, and skimmed the leaves off the swimming pool.

'This guy is bonkers and he's going to drive me bonkers,' Selby thought, as he watched the accountant cutting the grass. 'I can't stand this.'

When he'd finished with the housework Miles headed for the study but stopped to give Selby a pat.

'You look like a good dog,' he said. 'Let's see

if I can find some nice food for you in the fridge. I threw out those awful dog biscuits when I cleaned your bowl. I'm sure the Trifles won't mind.'

'I think I've just changed my mind about this guy,' Selby thought as Miles served him some slices of leftover roast and a bowl of bread and butter pudding with ice-cream on top. 'He's neat but he's nice.'

That afternoon Selby watched as Miles worked in the study, mumbling numbers and then shaking his head and saying things like, 'Goodness me,' and 'Tut tut.'

On he worked through the afternoon and into the evening.

'How's it going, Miles?' asked Dr Trifle at dinner.

'Getting there,' the man said. 'It'll be a few days till I know exactly what shape the council is in. Now if you'll both please excuse me, I really should get back to work.'

That night, while Dr and Mrs Trifle slept, Miles worked on and on, neatly writing numbers on pieces of paper. Early in the morning he took Selby for a walk and then had a breakfast of yogurt and cereal with the Trifles.

'I'll wash the breakfast dishes, Dr and Mrs Trifle,' Miles said. 'And I'll feed Selby. I'm sure you both have more important things to do.'

'Oh, Miles,' Mrs Trifle said, 'you really are a blessing.'

And wash the dishes he did. After that he cleaned the walls, patched a crack in the ceiling, and found some paint to touch up places where the paint was peeling.

'This guy fascinates me,' Selby thought. 'He must love putting things in order. I guess that's why he's a good accountant. I wonder what he does on his days off?'

And on Miles worked, and on, and on until Friday afternoon.

'I'm off for the weekend,' Miles announced. 'I should be able to finish the accounts on Monday but there's a special exhibition of pencils I wanted to see at the Museum of Accountancy in the city.'

'A pencil collection?' Dr Trifle asked.

'Oh, yes, and a wonderful one, too. I believe

they have a Birmingham Triangle from 1640. And it's never even been sharpened. There's also an ancient Babylonian clay tablet with a complete set of income tax figures from one thousand B.C.'

'That sounds very exciting,' Mrs Trifle said, yawning.

'Oh, it is, Mrs Trifle, it is. And you may also be excited to hear that I think the council will still have money left over after you pay all the bills.'

'That's wonderful news!' Mrs Trifle said. 'So we'll be able to pay you your fee.'

'Absolutely. But you should make sure that you save and budget from now on. Saving and budgeting, Mrs Trifle, those are the keys to everything. When I was a little boy my parents gave me an allowance of twenty cents a week. I calculated that if I saved it all and never spent a cent and if I could get a good interest rate then I could afford to buy a lovely pen and a pocket calculator by the time I was fourteen. And that's exactly what I did. Other children wasted their money on ice-creams and chocolates but not me. By the way, would you mind if I took Selby with me to the city? He'd be good company on the drive.'

'Selby? You want to take Selby with you for the weekend?'

'I'm sure he'll love my apartment. It's right on the beach.'

'Well, if you don't mind ...'

'Oh boy, oh boy!' Selby thought. 'This is going to be so much fun!'

Selby's first surprise was Miles's car. Parked about a block away was a fire engine-red sports car with exhaust pipes sticking through the bonnet. Miles let Selby in and then jumped in the driver's seat. In a second, the engine roared and the car flew off down the street, leaving a long black strip of rubber on the road.

'Yeeee — haaaa!' Miles screamed as he threw his coat and tie into the back seat. 'We've had enough work for the week, Selby. Let's party!'

'I can't believe this!' Selby squealed in his brain. 'One minute he's Mr Dull-and-Boring and next he's Mr Excitement!'

The apartment at the beach had everything Selby could wish for. It had a long curved balcony that looked out in every direction. And the furniture belonged in a mansion. The sun was just setting as Selby and Miles walked in.

Suddenly the lights in the apartment went on. Around them was a great crowd of people.

'Accountants rule!' someone screamed. 'Time to rage!'

'Hey, guys,' Miles said. 'Great to see you. Meet my dog-friend, Selby.'

'It's the weekend!' someone yelled. 'Let's dance!'

Into the night dance music blared and the accountants ate and drank and danced. And when they realised that Selby could move to the sound of music, he was the star of the party.

'I love accountants!' he said out loud — but it didn't matter because no one could hear him over the music. 'They really know how to have a great time.'

Soon waiters arrived with trays and trays of wonderful food.

'Try one of these,' Miles said, feeding Selby a peanut prawn. 'Hey, look at this, guys! The dog *loves* peanut prawns. I'm going to send out for a whole platter of them just for Selby!'

On the party went through the night but, finally, Selby couldn't stay awake anymore. He curled up on a fancy leather lounge and fell asleep.

In the morning the apartment was a mess: there were people still talking and dancing and others sleeping on the floor. Miles woke Selby up and took him for a walk along the beach before making him a huge breakfast of bacon and eggs and sausages.

'I love this!' Selby thought. 'If I didn't have the Trifles I'd want to be adopted by this guy.'

The next day Miles hired a speedboat and went deep-sea fishing with Selby and a group of his friends. Then they went up in a plane and flew around the city. They even went to the Pencil Exhibition at the Museum of Accountancy. Finally, back at the flat, everyone said goodbye.

'Thanks for another great weekend, Miles,' one of them said.

'I loved it, too,' Miles said. 'See you again next weekend.'

When they'd all gone and Miles and Selby were about to drive back to Bogusville, there was a loud knock at the door.

'Mr Manerd,' the man said, handing Miles an envelope, 'I'm Greg from A-1 Rentals. I'm afraid that I have to give you this eviction notice.'

'Eviction notice? You're kicking me out of this beautiful apartment?' Miles said.

'You know you're behind in your rent.'

'Please don't make me leave,' Miles pleaded. 'I've got a job and I'm about to get paid.'

'Well, I hope they're going to pay you lots of money because you're five months behind with your rent.'

'I'll pay you in a couple of days — honest.'

'I hope so,' the man said. 'Okay, I'll give you two days to come up with the money.'

Miles closed the door and opened a tall cupboard and threw in the envelope. But the cupboard was so full that piles and piles of envelopes and folders spilled out onto the floor. Some of the envelopes had things like FINAL NOTICE! and DEMAND PAYMENT and CAR PAYMENT DUE NOW! stamped on the front.

'Wow!' Selby thought. 'This guy's in worse trouble with his accounts than Mrs Trifle was.

He's an accountant but he can't look after his own money.'

'Oh, Selby,' Miles said, scooping up the papers and envelopes and piling them back into the cupboard, 'what am I going to do?'

The next morning, back in Bogusville, Miles washed the Trifles' breakfast dishes.

'I haven't quite finished my work on the council's accounts,' he said to Mrs Trifle. 'But I should have them done in an hour or so. I think you'll be surprised when you see how much money is in the council's bank account.'

'That's wonderful,' Mrs Trifle exclaimed.

'And here is the bill for my services.'

Mrs Trifle looked at it.

'That's very reasonable,' she said.

'Don't worry about writing a cheque. I'll just transfer the money directly from the council's bank account to mine and then I'll be off.'

'It's been a pleasure having you here,' Dr Trifle said. 'The house has never been this clean before.'

'You've done a wonderful job,' Mrs Trifle

said, giving him a huge hug. 'And I know that Selby has enjoyed your company.'

No sooner were the Trifles out the door than Miles turned on the computer.

'Now to transfer the money,' he said. 'Let's see, here's the account number and now to transfer . . .'

'Hey, hang on!' Selby thought as he looked at the computer screen. 'That's not the amount that he told Mrs Trifle. That's much much more.'

Miles got up and started pacing around the room.

'I can't do it,' he said out loud. 'I just can't do it. I'd hate myself too much. But I have to do it. Oh, Selby, what should I do?'

'You could start by not stealing the council's money,' Selby thought.

'If I don't do it then I'll lose my apartment, and my car — I'll lose everything! Oh, me. Oh, poor me!'

'Don't do it, Miles,' Selby pleaded in his brain. 'You're a good man, really. You've just let your life get out of control.'

'I'm a good man, really,' Miles said. 'But I'm a desperate man. I simply have to do it.'

Miles was about to push the RETURN button on the computer when he started pacing again.

'This is terrible!' Selby thought. 'I've got to do something — fast!'

Selby leapt up on the desk, knocking over a vase of flowers.

'Selby!' Miles cried. 'Now there's water all over the desk. Oh, well, I'll just finish this off first.'

Miles was about to hit the RETURN button again when he suddenly stopped.

'No, no, I can't do it — at least not with this mess here. I'll get a sponge.'

Miles went out to the kitchen.

'That's a start,' Selby thought. 'Now for the serious stuff. I've got to keep him from doing the evil deed.'

It was a diabolical dog that raced around the house, tipping over wastepaper baskets, furniture and flower pots and leaving greasy noseprints on the windows. By the time Miles returned with the sponge, there was mess everywhere.

'Selby! What are you doing?' cried the accountant, as he ran for a dustpan and brush.

'Oh, no! Now you've stepped in your water bowl and you're tracking dirt all over the place! What's got into you?'

It was a stealthy dog that picked up the telephone just when Miles turned on the vacuum cleaner in the other room.

'Is this Greg from A-1 Rentals?' Selby said, putting on his best accountant's voice. 'This is Miles, Miles Manerd. I think I have the answer to my financial problems. There are just a few things

I'd like you to do. And would you send me back an email about it? Here's the address ...'

It was a relaxed dog that lay innocently on the carpet in the study when the mild-mannered accountant returned.

'Now for the terrible deed,' he said, 'sitting down at the computer. What's this? An email? For me? Let's see what it says.'

And this is what it said:

DEAR MILES,

I HAVE DONE AS YOU INSTRUCTED. I THINK IT WAS VERY SENSIBLE FOR YOU TO GIVE UP THAT APARTMENT. I'VE FOUND A SMALLER ONE FOR YOU WHICH YOU CAN MOVE INTO STRAIGHT AWAY. THE CAR RENTAL AGENCY IS HAPPY FOR YOU TO EXCHANGE YOURS FOR AN OLDER ONE. AND THE SALE OF HALF YOUR FURNITURE — IT WOULDN'T HAVE FITTED INTO THE SMALLER FLAT ANYWAY, AS YOU SAID — SHOULD PAY YOUR EXISTING BILLS AND THE RENT YOU OWE ME.

BEST WISHES,

GREG

'Did as I instructed? I don't remember asking him to do anything but I must have. And it's the answer to all my problems!' Miles cried. 'Sometimes I amaze myself. Now if I work hard and save and budget everything will be fine. I'll just pay myself what the council owes me now.'

Selby watched as the accountant transferred the right amount of money.

'Goodbye, Selby,' he said, giving Selby a pat. 'You were a very naughty dog just then but you kept me from making a terrible mistake. You'll never know how much you helped me.'

'No,' Selby thought, as the accountant walked to his car, '*you're* the one who will never know how much I helped you. Goodbye and good luck.'

'Let's talk about school holidays,' the man on the radio said. 'Do kids need breaks from school? If you have any thoughts on this, give us a ring. This is Mike Balistik, known around here as Magic Mike, coming to you from Radio OK4U, the Heart of the Bush.'

'Hey, I like the sound of this guy,' Selby thought, as he lay in the lounge room listening to the radio.

'Why do we pay for schools and then leave them empty for months of the year?' Mike continued. 'Wouldn't kids learn more if they went to school every day?'

'Good point, Mike,' Selby thought.

'And what do kids do on holidays? Nothing.

They watch TV. They sleep-in in the morning. Parents have to miss work to stay at home and look after them. They waste their time — and everyone else's. Do they learn anything on their holidays? Of course not.'

'That's true,' Selby thought. 'I hadn't ever considered that.'

'And when they leave the house it's to get into trouble. I say keep them in school and out of trouble. Okay, do we have any callers on the line, Richard?'

'Putting Laurence through, Mike.'

'Hello, Laurence.'

'Hello, Magic Mike, I love your show,' a man said. 'It's so great to hear someone who's not afraid to speak his mind.'

'Thanks, Laurence. There isn't enough of it these days, is there?'

'That's for sure. Mike, you know how you were saying that kids should always go to school and that? Over in Bogusville some kids were on school holidays and they went back to their school and broke a window.'

'Is that right, Laurence? Well, it wouldn't happen if we kept them in school. Thanks for that, Laurence. (*Click*) Anyone else on the line, Richard?'

'I remember that broken window,' Selby thought. 'Willy and Billy did it and boy did they get into trouble!'

'We've got Camilla on the line, Mike.'

'Hello, Camilla. What do you think about getting rid of school holidays?'

'Mr Balistik, I'm a teacher and I think that kids need time off from school. They need to get away from school work to get their energy back.'

'Hey, that sounds like Camilla Bonzer,' Selby thought, 'the librarian at Bogusville Primary School. She's got a point.'

'Do you know what, Camilla?' Magic Mike said. 'I think you're wrong. You just want the kids to have holidays so *you* can have lots of holidays.'

'No, don't you see how important it is —'

'I can see all right! I can see that you're an idiot! An idiot who only cares about yourself!'

'But–but–but —'

'But nothing. You'd let the kids off for half the year if it was up to you.'

'No, I wouldn't. It's just that —'

'Yes, you would! You'd have them going to school for one month every year so that you could go on holidays for the rest of the time. Well, it's just not good enough. There are people who are right and there are people who are wrong and you are wrong wrong *wrong*, lady! Wake up to yourself! Cut her off, Richard, she's an idiot.'

(*Click*)

'What's wrong with me?' Mike said with a sigh. 'I just think that people ought to do a good day's work for a good day's pay.'

'Now wait, Mike,' Selby thought. 'Camilla had a point. You didn't even listen to her side of it.'

'And now let's talk about dogs,' Mike went on. 'Filthy, nasty, flea-bitten, dangerous creatures — a bunch of do-nothings that poop all over footpaths. Why don't we all get together and round them up and shoot them? Anyone out there want to talk about dogs?'

'I do, Mike,' Selby said, grabbing the phone and dialling Radio OK4U. 'My name's Sel — Selig. May I speak to Magic Mike, please?'

'Putting you through.'

'Mike, is that you?'

'What is it, Selig?'

'About dogs being filthy and nasty, and dangerous and that.'

'What about it?'

'Well, we're not all like that —'

'We?' Mike laughed. 'Did you say, we? Like you're a dog or something?'

'No, sorry, I meant *they*. You see most of what you say is really the owners' fault, not the dogs' fault.'

'Wrong, Selig! Cut this guy off, Richard!'

'Let me explain,' Selby went on. 'Take fleas for example —'

'Cut him off!'

'— the only thing dogs can do about fleas is scratch. And that doesn't get rid of them. Only the owners can get flea medicine.'

'Richard, cut this idiot off!'

'A dog can't just walk into a vet's surgery and say, "I'd like some Flea-Off," and then hand over the money, now can he?'

'Richard, if you don't hang up on this fool then I quit!'

'Hear him out, Mike,' Richard said. 'I like the sound of this guy.'

'The only sound I'd like from this guy is the sound of my foot on his backside,' Mike said.

'And as for dogs being do-nothings,' Selby continued. 'Where would farmers be without sheep and cattle dogs? Where would blind people be without guide dogs?'

'Most dogs don't do anything, Selig. What a stupid name — Selig. Richard, I'm warning you. Cut him off or I'm outta here!'

'Dogs,' Selby said calmly, 'are faithful and loyal and loving and kind. They are the most wonderful creatures on earth. And why do I say this, Mike? Because they make people happy.'

'Richard!'

'Can you think of anything better than making people happy? Do you have any idea what might happen if we got rid of dogs?'

'Okay, I'm outta here! You can take this stupid show and do whatever you want with it, Richie, old boy, because I'm heading back to the city! Goodbye and good riddance to all of you flyblown bush-bunnies.'

(*Slam!*)

Selby went on and on talking about the friendship between dogs and their owners. When he was finished Richard's voice said, 'Thank you for your call today, Selig. Could you hold while we go to a commercial?'

'Sure.'

As the song for the Dry-Mouth Dog Biscuits ad came on the radio, Selby heard Richard's voice again.

'Hi, Selig, this is Richard here, the producer. We're not on air now. I wanted to say that you were very good. You have a great way with words.'

'It's just that I feel very strongly about dogs,' Selby explained.

'You probably feel strongly about a lot of things,' the producer said. 'Quite frankly I'm glad to see the end of Mike. He was getting very boring. We were losing our audience. Besides, how dumb is it to attack dogs when the Dry-Mouth Dog Biscuit Company pays for ads on this show? Get me?'

'I think so,' Selby said, not really sure that he did.

'Now, Selig, I have an offer for you. How

would you like to be the new Magic Mike? We'll call you Silvertone Selig, because you're a smooth talker.'

'Oh, no, I couldn't possibly.'

'You're good, Selig. Already the switchboard is flooded with calls from people who love you.'

'Really? No, the thing is I have a bit of a problem with my appearance.'

'Are you ugly or something? This is radio, Selig. No one will see you,' Selby said.

'No one but you,' Selby said.

'Oh, I get it,' the producer said. 'You want to keep your privacy, don't you? You don't want people to find out who you really are or where you live because they'd ruin your life forever.'

'Spot on,' Selby said.

'Selig probably isn't even your real name.'

'Right again.'

'I don't care who you really are or where you live, just come in here with a bag over your head and do the radio show. How does that sound?'

'It could be fun,' Selby said. 'I'll think about it.'

★ ★ ★

It was a strange sight. Standing at the studio door was what looked like a man in a dog suit. But of course we know that it wasn't a man in a dog suit but a *dog* in a dog suit — Selby's disguise.

'That's perfect!' Richard said, shaking a paw of the dog suit, little knowing that there was a real paw inside. 'No wonder you like dogs — you are one! Have a seat, Selig, you're on the air.'

Selby looked around nervously. On the other side of the glass the producer was telling him to start talking.

'Hello, folks,' Selby started, 'I'm your new DJ, Silvertone Selig. What don't we like? I don't know about you but I don't like people who spit on the ground.'

The producer nodded and put the first caller through.

'Hi there, Silvertone,' the man said. 'This spitting business: I wouldn't spit if anyone was looking but if there's no one there, what does it matter?'

'It's not just about people seeing you spit,' Selby said. 'It's about germs. When you spit, germs go into the air and into the ground water and someone else can catch them.'

In the first commercial break, Richard said, 'That was great, Selig. What are you going to talk about next?'

'I don't know,' Selby said. 'How about chocolate?'

'What about it?'

'It's bad for dogs.'

'Forget dogs. We've done them. What else?'

'I could say that a little bit can be good for people but too much can be bad,' Selby said. 'Something like that?'

'No, Selig, take my advice — you *hate* chocolate.'

'I do?'

'You do,' Richard said. 'People want strength, energy, strong opinions, Selig. They don't want "on the one hand this and on the other hand that". They want to know what makes you angry. Now why do you hate chocolate?'

'I don't know,' Selby said. 'At the movies people sometimes unwrap crinkly chocolate wrappers and make too much noise.'

'Good one,' Richard said. 'Keep it up. You're on in five, four, three, two, one ...'

The producer pointed to Selby.

'This is Silvertone Selig here and I *hate* chocolate,' Selby said. 'Sticky brown mucky stuff. What do *you* think? Do we have anyone on the line, Richard?'

'I've got Emily here, Selig.'

'Hi there, Selig,' Emily said. 'I like you much better than that Mike guy.'

'Thanks, Em,' Selby said. 'What do you think about chocolate?'

'I don't mind it, Selig. And I like chocolate ice-cream, too.'

'Have you ever had a chocolate bar melt in your pocket?' Selby asked.

'Well, yes, once. It made a terrible mess and I got into heaps of trouble.'

'There you go,' Selby said. 'And you do know that too much chocolate can ruin your teeth and make you fat?'

'That's true,' Emily said. 'I guess you're right, Selig.'

'How was that?' Selby asked the producer in the next break.

'It was good, Selig, but try to get to the point. Say, "You love chocolate but look at yourself: you're fat and your teeth are falling out!"'

'But what if she's thin and her teeth are okay?'

'Don't worry, I'll cut her off before she can say it and then you get stuck into her when she can't answer. It's an old trick of the trade.'

'I'm not sure about this, Richard,' Selby said.

'Okay, it's up to you, Selig. But here's something that'll make you boiling mad. There are some people trying to rip off country people.'

'Really? How?'

'They're running a raffle. Buy a ticket and you win a car.'

'That sounds okay,' Selby said.

'What they're really out to do is to con people into buying lots of raffle tickets. Sure, the winner gets the car. But who gets the rest of the money? It goes straight into the greedy little pockets of the organisers.'

'That's terrible,' Selby said. 'That makes me really mad.'

'I thought it would. It's called the BHB Raffle. You're on in three, two, one ...'

'This is Radio OK4U and this is Silvertone Selig,' Selby said. 'I've just learnt about a raffle called the BHB Raffle. Well, folks, it ought to be called the RO Raffle because it's a *rip-off*. Does anyone want to talk about this?'

A moment later the producer told Selby that Mrs Smith was on the phone.

'You're on the air, Mrs Smith,' Selby said.

'I just wanted to say that the BHB Raffle is a good thing. In fact, I'm one of the organisers and —'

'Ahah!' Selby said. 'And you want to collect much more money than the cost of the car?'

'That's true but —'

'And then you keep the extra money, don't you?'

'Well, that's not exactly —'

'And your name probably isn't even Mrs Smith.'

'No, it isn't but —'

'Cut her off, Richard!' Selby boomed. 'I've heard enough from this greedy, selfish woman!'

(*Click*)

'She's just out for herself and her mates. All she wants to do is take your hard-earned money so she won't have to do a good day's work for a good day's pay. Well, I hate it. And I know you do, too.'

The producer made a wind-up signal with his finger in the air.

'And that's all from me, Silvertone Selig. I'll catch you again tomorrow.'

'That was excellent!' the producer said when the program finished. 'You made short work of that lying woman. You're a natural.'

'I kind of enjoyed it,' Selby admitted. 'It's fun getting all angry. Do you really want me to do it again tomorrow?'

'Absolutely! And the day after that and the day after that. If you keep going like this, everyone will want to advertise on this show. We'll be rich! We can talk about money tomorrow. Hey, how about taking off the dog suit so I can see who you really are?'

'I'm really a dog,' Selby said. 'A dog in a dog suit.'

'You're what?' the producer looked puzzled and then he burst into laughter. 'A dog in a dog suit. That's a good one. See you tomorrow, Silvertone.'

That evening, Selby was lying on the carpet in the Trifles' lounge room thinking of what he was going to say the next day on his radio show. Mrs Trifle came in late from a meeting at the council. There were tears in her eyes.

'What's wrong?' Dr Trifle asked.

'Oh, I don't know. Everything is just too hard,' she said. 'And people can be so mean.'

'Mean?'

'Yes, I rang up the radio station today about the BHB Raffle — you know, the Bush Hospitals' Benefit.'

'Oh, no!' Selby thought. 'Mrs Smith was really Mrs Trifle!'

'Why?' Dr Trifle asked.

'The hospitals really need money to keep going,' Mrs Trifle sniffed. 'But instead of helping us, this new presenter attacked me.'

'Gulp,' Selby gulped. 'Oh, no, what have I done?'

'He attacked me and he attacked the raffle,' Mrs Trifle said. 'We've only sold eight dollars in tickets so far and now no one's going to buy any more. We'll have to give away the car and we'll end up losing thousands and thousands of dollars. And it was my idea for the raffle.'

'Poor Mrs Trifle,' Selby thought, as he lay

wide awake through the night. 'And it's all my fault. I got in front of that microphone and I suddenly got angry. I think I got mike rage! Oh, woe woe woe.'

The next day, Selby went to the radio station again.

'What are you going to talk about today?' the producer asked.

'The raffle,' Selby answered.

'Do you have something new to say about it?'

'Yes, I certainly do.'

'Okay, coming up now ... five, four, three, two, one ...'

'This is Radio OK4U, coming to you from the Heart of the Bush and this is Silvertone Selig. Yesterday I talked about the BHB Raffle — only I was wrong, folks. I don't mind admitting that I was wrong.'

Selby watched as the shocked producer opened the door into the studio.

'What are you saying?' he whispered.

'BHB stands for ... Bush Hospitals' Benefit,' Selby went on. 'The hospitals are in desperate need of money and the raffle is to raise that money.'

'Selig, they don't want to hear that!'

'So if you can possibly afford it, please buy as many tickets as you can. You could win a car, but even if you don't, the money is all going to a worthy cause.'

'And I'm going to turn your mike off!' Richard yelled.

'Oh, no, you're not!' Selby said, covering the switch with both paws. 'And another thing, listeners,' he went on, 'if you have a dog, don't buy him — or her — Dry-Mouth Dog Biscuits. They're mostly sawdust. I know, I've eaten tonnes of them!'

'You what? You're killing us, Silvertone!' the producer screamed. 'Who are you, anyway? I'm going to find out just who you are!'

The producer grabbed the head of Selby's dog suit and started pulling.

'You get your hands off me!' Selby yelled.

Selby put his paws on top of his head but the producer was too strong for him. Slowly, the head of the dog suit came off.

'A dog!' the producer gasped. 'What a

disguise! You put on a dog suit — and then you put on another dog suit! Now let's see who you really are!' he said, grabbing Selby's real head and trying to pull it off. 'Ouch! You bit me!' he screamed, falling backward as Selby made for the door. 'I can't believe this! I've been bitten by the head of a dog suit!'

'And you're lucky,' Selby thought, as he raced for home to hide the suit under the house again, 'that I didn't bite *your* head off!'

# SUPERSTITIOUS SELBY

'Did you know that it's supposed to be good luck to carry around a rabbit's foot?' Dr Trifle said, looking up from the book he was reading.

'I don't believe it,' said Mrs Trifle.

'I don't either,' thought Selby. 'It wasn't good luck for the rabbit — he had four of them and look what happened to *him*.'

'Did you know that if you spill pepper you'll have an argument with your best friend?' Dr Trifle said, turning the page. 'And if you dream about a lizard you have a secret enemy.'

'I dreamt about a lizard once,' Selby thought, 'so I must have a secret enemy. It could be Willy or Billy but there's no secret about them.'

'If your nose itches it means that you'll be kissed by a fool,' Dr Trifle said.

'Come to think of it,' Mrs Trifle said, 'my nose itched just before you kissed me yesterday.'

'Is that true?'

'No, just kidding, dear. Right now all I care about is collecting the money for the Bush Hospitals' Benefit Raffle. We've asked everyone who wants tickets to leave the money in their mailbox by ten o'clock tonight. You and I have to collect it and give it to Camilla. She'll be drawing the winner tomorrow morning at the Hospitals' Benefit Breakfast. And, thanks to that nice man on the radio, lots of people are buying lots of tickets. The winner will get a new car and there should be heaps of money left over for Bogusville Hospital.'

'Did you say that *you and I* have to collect the money? Aren't Melanie Mildew and Postie Paterson going to help?'

'Melanie is sick,' Mrs Trifle said, filling out a raffle ticket for herself and putting it with some money in an envelope. 'She caught a cold in the rain. She blames herself. She thinks that *she* made it rain.'

'What do you mean?'

'You know the saying that if you kill a spider it will rain? Well, she killed one in her garage last week.'

'If that saying was true,' Selby thought, 'there wouldn't be one spider left in Bogusville. The farmers would have killed them all to make it rain.'

'What's wrong with Postie?' Dr Trifle asked.

'He fell down and hurt his back just after a black cat crossed his path.'

'Yes, they say that's bad luck,' Dr Trifle said, opening his book again. 'There are so many superstitions. Did you know that if your cheeks feel like they're on fire it means someone is talking about you?'

'The last time I felt like my cheeks were on fire,' Selby thought, 'they were. I was standing too close to the heater.'

'What is that book you're reading?' Mrs Trifle asked.

'It's called *Half Your Luck*. It's by our friend Madame Mascara,' Dr Trifle said. 'She's a very superstitious woman.'

'And a very rich one,' Mrs Trifle said. 'She's

had an incredible run of good luck.'

'Here's another one,' Dr Trifle said. '*Step on a crack and break your mother's back.*'

'If that was true,' Selby thought, 'every mother in the world would be walking around with a broken back.'

'That actually did happen to a girl at my primary school,' Mrs Trifle said.

'You mean she stepped on a crack and broke her mother's back?'

'Not exactly. She tripped on a crack and fell on her mother and hurt her mother's back.'

'Not quite the same,' Dr Trifle said, 'but it was certainly bad luck for her mother. Did you know it was also bad luck if you let milk boil over?'

'I knew that,' Selby said. 'Last year Mrs Trifle let some milk boil over and it splashed on me. It nearly killed me!'

'I knew that,' Mrs Trifle said. 'I boiled some milk over and a drop or two hit Selby. But he didn't seem to notice.'

'Madame Mascara's book says that you should never have the head of your bed pointing north,' Dr Trifle said.

'Oh, give me a break,' Selby thought.

'We moved the bedroom furniture last week,' Mrs Trifle said. 'Hmmm. Let's just have a look at it.'

Selby followed the Trifles into the bedroom.

'Just as I thought,' Mrs Trifle said. 'It's pointing north. And, look, you left your hat lying on the bed. That's very bad luck — or so they say.'

'And so are shoes lying upside down on the floor,' Dr Trifle added. 'Both of yours are upside down.'

'I think we both got out of the wrong side of the bed this morning,' Mrs Trifle said, with a laugh. 'What is the wrong side of a bed, anyway?'

'Madame Mascara explains this,' Dr Trifle said. 'The wrong side is the side you didn't get in on.'

'Then it's true,' Mrs Trifle said. 'I did get out of bed on the wrong side this morning.'

'Do you really believe this nonsense?' Dr Trifle asked. 'I don't.'

'Neither do I,' Mrs Trifle said. 'Besides, what is bad luck? What could possibly happen?'

'A plane could crash into our house,' Dr Trifle said. 'But what would be the chance of that?'

Suddenly in the distance there was the sound of an approaching aeroplane. Dr and Mrs Trifle listened for a moment.

'Highly unlikely,' Mrs Trifle said, as she turned over her shoes. 'But I do think my shoes look better right-side up.'

'And my hat shouldn't be on the bed,' Dr Trifle said, snatching it up.

'And I think I did like the bed better round the other way,' Mrs Trifle said, as the plane passed overhead. 'Didn't you?'

'Absolutely,' Dr Trifle said. 'Let's move everything back the way it was.'

'Hang on. You don't suppose we're superstitious, do you?' Mrs Trifle asked.

'Of course not. But there are lots of mysterious things we don't know about. We're just not taking any chances. That's different.'

'Oh, please,' Selby thought, as he headed for the lounge room. 'This is getting totally out of hand. I've got to do something to stop this nonsense before they drive themselves crazy — and me, too! Hey, I know . . .'

Selby raced around the house while the Trifles were rearranging the bedroom.

'Phew!' Dr Trifle sighed, as he and Mrs Trifle came back to the lounge room. 'Now to collect that raffle money. Oops, someone's spilt salt on the table. That's bad luck.'

'I wonder who did that?' Mrs Trifle said, taking a pinch of it and throwing it over her left shoulder. 'This should make it good luck again.'

Mrs Trifle grabbed her handbag but, just as she did, her hand mirror fell to the floor and broke.

'Oh, no! A broken mirror! Seven years' bad luck,' Mrs Trifle said. 'How did that happen? I thought I'd closed my handbag.'

'Hang on,' Dr Trifle said, thumbing through the book. 'There's something you can do. Here it is: Turn around three times, scream, "Shoot me! Shoot me! I'm a rooster!" and then spit.'

'But that's too silly,' Mrs Trifle said.

'I agree. Don't do it. Better to risk a bit of bad luck.'

'Shoot me! Shoot me! I'm a rooster!' Mrs Trifle said.

Then she spat, narrowly missing Selby.

'Maybe that wasn't such a good idea,' Dr Trifle said. 'It says in the book that it's very bad luck to spit on the floor.'

'Is there anything I can do about it?' Mrs Trifle asked, wiping the floor with a tissue.

'It says here that you have to stand on your head and stay there for a minute.'

'This is getting really *really* stupid!' Selby thought, as Mrs Trifle got down on all fours.

'I can't get my feet up in the air,' she said.

Dr Trifle lifted Mrs Trifle's legs up in the air, waited for a minute and then let her down again.

'Phew! I'm glad that's over,' Selby thought.

'Phew! I'm glad that's over,' Mrs Trifle said. 'Now let's go.'

Dr Trifle opened the front door and then stopped.

'We can't go out,' he said, looking at the ladder that was propped up outside the door. 'We can't go out or we'll walk under the ladder. That's very bad luck. I wonder how it got there?'

'Oh, for pity's sake!' Selby thought. 'Just go under it and you'll see that it isn't bad luck after all!'

'You must have been cleaning leaves out of the gutter,' Mrs Trifle said. 'And you left the ladder there. Let's go out the back door.'

They started for the back door.

'Wait,' Mrs Trifle said. 'It's bad luck if you don't leave a house through the same door that you came in.'

'Yes, that's in this book, too,' Dr Trifle said. 'But it's okay because you were in the back-yard when I came home so you came in through the back door and you can go out through the back door. I didn't, I came in through the front door.'

'So what do we do?'

'Simple: You go out the back and then jump the fence into the laneway, run around the house and move the ladder. Then I can go out the front door and everything will be okay.'

'This is amazing!' Selby thought. 'What's the problem? Just go out and collect that money!'

'Everything *would* be okay,' Mrs Trifle said. 'But there's no way I can jump that back fence. Unless ... you could go out the front and bring the ladder in and then I'll take it out the back and put it up to the fence for me to climb over. Then you can go out the front again and run around and help me down the other side.'

'But to do that, I'll have to go under the ladder first,' Dr Trifle reminded her. 'So it won't work. Besides, you and I should never go out different doors when we're leaving the house. *Leave together, stay together. Leave apart, stay apart.*'

'I couldn't stand it if we ever stayed apart,' Mrs Trifle sighed.

'I couldn't either,' Dr Trifle said. 'But I don't know what to do because we have to collect that money. I say we just forget all this superstition stuff.'

'I agree,' Mrs Trifle said. 'Let's go.'

'Finally!' Selby thought. 'They're coming to their senses. It's about time!'

Mrs Trifle suddenly noticed the calendar on the wall.

'Oh, no! Do you know what day it is? It's Friday the thirteenth! The unluckiest day of the year! That's the last straw. I'm not going anywhere. I'm going straight to bed and staying there till tomorrow.'

'I guess I'd better do the same,' Dr Trifle sighed. 'At least we'll be safe now that our bed's pointing in the right direction.'

'Now I've really done it!' Selby squealed in his brain. 'I was only trying to cure them and now I've made it worse! They're never going to collect the raffle money! What am I going to do? I guess *I'll* have to collect the money!'

That night was the busiest night of Selby's life. He ran from mailbox to mailbox, quietly opening them and taking out the envelopes with the money. He filled bag after bag with

tickets and money and left them in a pile on Camilla Bonzer's doorstep.

'I never thought money could be so heavy!' Selby thought as he dragged the last bag of money and tickets to the pile. 'I'm exhausted! And I've finished just in time, the sun is coming up. But what am I going to do about the Trifles?'

Selby limped back to the house, curled up and fell asleep. He woke to the sound of the telephone ringing. Mrs Trifle stumbled out of the bedroom to answer it.

'Camilla, I'm terribly sorry...' she started. 'What?... What do you mean?... Really?... No!... No!! ... *No*!!! That's wonderful! I can't wait to tell my husband!'

'What is it?' Dr Trifle asked. 'What's happened?'

'That was Camilla phoning from the Hospitals' Benefit Breakfast. Apparently someone collected all the raffle money.'

'I guess Postie and Melanie must have felt well enough after all,' Dr Trifle said. 'Hey, if Postie was okay then do you know what that means?'

'No, what?'

'Maybe black cats aren't such bad luck after all.'

'And the very best news of all,' Mrs Trifle said, 'is that I won!'

'You what?'

'My ticket won the raffle! I won a new car! Can you believe it?'

'No, because you didn't even send your raffle ticket in,' Dr Trifle said, looking to where the envelope had been on the table and not seeing it. 'That was more than luck — that was a miracle! The ticket got to the raffle all by itself! You see, didn't I say that there are lots of mysterious things that we don't know about?'

'You can say that again,' Selby thought.

'Of course I won't keep the car,' Mrs Trifle said.

'You won't?'

'No, it wouldn't look right for the mayor to win the prize. I'll tell them to sell it and give the money to the hospital.'

'It seems that all of those things that were supposed to be bad luck, weren't bad luck after all,' Dr Trifle said.

'Good!' Selby thought. 'Finally all that silly superstition business is over.'

'In fact, they were *good* luck,' Mrs Trifle said. 'Quick, let's move the bed back and walk under that ladder and — hey, it wasn't Friday the thirteenth after all! Someone must have flipped the calendar over to next month. Oh, goody, there's a Friday the thirteenth at the end of next week!'

'Great,' Dr Trifle said, spilling a pile of salt and looking around for another mirror to break. 'Now how are we going to get a black cat to cross our path?'

'Oh, woe woe woe,' Selby thought. 'This is going to be just as bad as before. Just my luck ... what am I saying?!'

# DOG TALK
### by Selby Trifle

I wish that I could learn to speak
In German, Portuguese and Greek
And Arabic and Japanese
And Hindi, Thai and Cantonese.
I wish my tongue could wrap around
Every sort of foreign sound
From Timbuktu to Samarkand
And even EuroDisneyland.
Yes, I would stop and say, 'G'day!'
To all the folks who came my way.
They'd say, with faces all agog,
'He talks like us! – and he's a dog!'

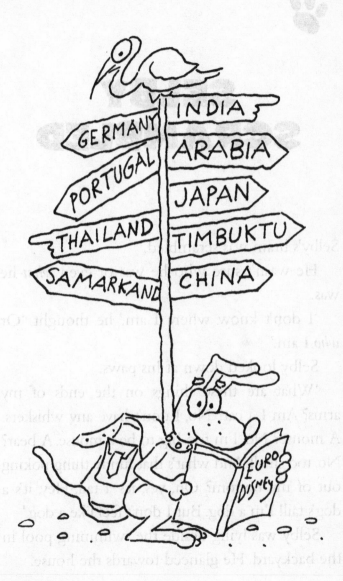

# SELBY SCRAMBLED

Selby's brain was scrambled.

He wasn't sure who he was or even *what* he was.

'I don't know where I am,' he thought. 'Or *who* I am.'

Selby looked down at his paws.

'What are these things on the ends of my arms? Am I a cat? No, I don't have any whiskers. A mouse? No, I'm too big to be a mouse. A bear? No, too small. And what's that funny thing poking out of my bottom? Oh, yes, it's a tail. Hey, it's a dog's tail! I'm a dog. But I don't feel like a dog.'

Selby was lying beside the swimming pool in the backyard. He glanced towards the house.

Suddenly the back door opened. Walking towards him was something strange — a machine, maybe.

'It's shaped kind of like a person,' Selby thought, 'but it's all shiny. People aren't shiny. No, it can't be a person. Besides, people don't have flashing lights all over their chests.'

The creature came closer. It was humming.

'He's humming that song. I know that song but I can't remember where I've heard it before. Oh, I'm so confused.'

Selby's problems had all begun a week before. Mrs Trifle was at work and Dr Trifle was in his workroom. Selby was secretly reading the fantasy series, *Valley of Dead Souls*. He'd just started the last book, *Dogboy's Final Challenge*.

'I can't wait to see if Dogboy kills the Gork king,' Selby thought. 'It's *sooooooo* exciting!'

Selby was so caught up in his book that he barely heard Mrs Trifle's footsteps and the sound of the front door opening. Selby quickly slipped the book under the lounge just as Dr Trifle came out of his workroom.

'How was your day, dear?' Dr Trifle asked his wife.

'Terrible,' she sighed. 'Problems, problems, problems. After a while I was so confused and exhausted that, before I knew it, I'd eaten a whole bag of leftover chocolate Easter eggs. And everyone was giggling at me because I kept humming that song from the Dry-Mouth Dog Biscuits ad without even thinking.'

'What song is that?'

'You remember, it goes like this:

*Oh Dry-Mouth, oh Dry-Mouth oh wiggley woo*
*Dry and delicious so crunchy to chew*
*Fill up my bowl with my fave-ourite food*
*And if you do so – then I'll love you too.*

'I hate that song but it's stuck in my head. It's embarrassing when I hum it!'

'I hate it, too,' Selby thought, 'and it's stuck in my head, too. But if *I* start humming it, it's going to be more than embarrassing.'

'I don't understand the human brain,' Mrs Trifle said. 'We think we're logical and sensible and then we gobble up whole bags of chocolate Easter eggs and sing dog food ads without even thinking. And we make so many mistakes.'

'What we need are helpers that *don't* make mistakes,' Dr Trifle said.

'Yes, that would be perfect — but impossible.'

'Impossible? Never say *impossible* to an inventor,' Dr Trifle said. 'Frank! Come here!'

There was a rattle and a *clunk* in the workroom and then a *clomp clomp clomp*. The door opened and there stood a strange shiny machine the size and shape of a man.

'What's that?' Mrs Trifle screamed.

'It's Frank, my newly invented robot.'

'Your robot? What a strange-looking thing. He looks a bit ... well, scary. I'll bet you named him after Frankenstein's monster.'

'Frankenstein's monster? Goodness, no. Frank stands for Fully Responsive Animated Neutronic Kinematoid. F-R-A-N-K. Listen to this. Hello Frank.'

'Hello ... mister ... man,' Frank said slowly.

'Call me Dr Trifle. And this is Mrs Trifle.'

'Hello ... Dr Trifle ... and ... Mrs Trifle.'

'That's amazing!' Mrs Trifle gasped. 'He just learnt our names.'

'Frank has a special chip in him that lets him learn,' Dr Trifle said. 'Speak a little faster, Frank.'

'*HowfastItalkyouisthisokay*?'

'No, slow down a bit.'

'Me say you: how fast I talk you. Is this okay?'

'That's a good speed but you have to learn to speak properly,' Dr Trifle said, grabbing a book from the bookshelf called *English Grammar*. 'Here, read this.'

Frank took the book and fanned through the pages so fast that Selby could feel the breeze.

'What's he doing?' Selby wondered.

'What did he just do?' Mrs Trifle asked.

'He just read the book,' Dr Trifle said. 'Here, Frank, now read this dictionary, please.'

The robot fanned the pages of a huge dictionary then handed it back.

'He can't have read the whole thing,' Mrs Trifle said.

'Yes, Madam, you can be assured that I did,' Frank said. 'Test me on my knowledge if you care to do so. How about the word *grampus*?'

'Did he say *grandpa*?' Selby thought. 'Everyone knows what grandpa means.'

'*Grampus*,' Frank said. 'A member of the dolphin family found mostly in the northern seas such as —'

'That's enough, Frank,' Dr Trifle said. 'Get a chair for Mrs Trifle.'

'Yes, sir.'

Frank started towards a chair but Dr Trifle's leg shot out, sending the robot crashing to the ground and narrowly missing Selby.

'What in heaven's name did you do that for?' Mrs Trifle asked, helping the robot to his feet. 'That was cruel!'

'No, it wasn't,' Dr Trifle said. 'Frank, I said, get a chair for Mrs Trifle.'

Once again, the robot walked towards the chair and once again, Dr Trifle's leg shot out but this time the robot walked around it.

'You see? He can learn from experience. Now he will always be aware of someone trying to trip him,' Dr Trifle explained. 'If Frank had a mind like us he'd soon forget and you could trip him again and again. That's the wonderful thing about him — he's not a person. You can't hurt his feelings, because he doesn't *have* feelings. And he's a perfect servant because he does as he's told and he won't get cranky when we order him around.'

'Are you sure you didn't damage him when you tripped him?'

'Goodness, no. He's as tough as old boots. In time he'll learn to do everything — well, everything except swim,' Dr Trifle laughed. 'He's a bit too heavy for that.'

'I think I like this robot,' Selby thought. 'He can't swim either — just like me.'

'You are a very clever man, dear,' Mrs Trifle said. 'But right now I really must make dinner.'

'Why don't you just relax and take it easy? Frank, make dinner.'

'I would be pleased to,' the robot said, 'but I'm afraid that it would be metempirical.'

'Metem — what?' Selby thought.

'Metem — what?' Dr Trifle asked.

'Metempirical. Outside my experience. I've never made dinner before.'

'Oh, I see,' Dr Trifle said with a laugh. 'First of all, Frank, please use smaller words when you talk to us. And, secondly, there are cookery books in the kitchen. Just find some recipes and follow the instructions.'

'Yes, sir.'

'This guy is amazing!' Selby thought, as Dr and Mrs Trifle relaxed in front of the television while Frank worked in the kitchen. 'He's just read every cookery book on that shelf! Look! He's heating up a frying pan. I wonder what he's going to put in it.'

Frank suddenly turned and came straight for Selby, picking him up in his robot arms.

'Hey! Let me go!' Selby thought. 'What's this guy doing? I can't get loose!'

Selby let out a howl and then started barking as loudly as he could.

'Frank!' Mrs Trifle screamed. 'What are you doing?'

'I was going to make a hot dog,' Frank said.

'A hotdog isn't a hot *dog*,' Mrs Trifle explained, taking Selby out of the robot's arms. 'It's a kind of sausage. And we don't have any so make something else.'

'Do you have a fish with hands then? If you do then I could make fish fingers.'

'Frank, fish fingers aren't fish *fingers*, they're just pieces of fish that are long and thin like fingers. Make something else, please, and don't interrupt us again.'

'That guy almost killed me!' Selby thought. 'It's a good thing the Trifles were here. But hang on, if they were away *I* could have told him not to cook me. In fact, when the Trifles are out of the house, I can boss Frank around. I think I like this guy again.'

Selby could hardly keep from laughing when dinner was finally served.

'Frank,' Mrs Trifle said. 'What is this frozen stew?'

'That's chilly, Madam.'

'Chilli is supposed to be hot, not chilly. And what about the salad? It tasted okay but what were those dirty socks and underwear doing in it? That's *not* how you dress a salad, Frank. And, as for the dessert, sponge cake is not made from sponges.'

'I'm terribly, terribly sorry, Madam,' Frank said. 'But don't worry, I've got a mud cake in the oven.'

'Mud cake?' Mrs Trifle said, sniffing the air. 'Oh, yuck! Don't even tell me! Oh, Frank, you have a lot to learn about cooking.'

But Frank did learn — and learn and learn.

Soon he'd read every book in the house, including all thirty volumes of the encyclopedia, and was downloading information from the internet directly into his memory. His cooking got to be fantastic and he learnt to cut the grass, take telephone messages and clean the house.

'This guy is great,' Selby thought. 'I could tell the Trifles my secret now and they wouldn't put me to work. Frank is already doing all those boring things that I was afraid they'd make me do. But what if other people found out about me? There would be TV camera crews around the house all the time and people trying to dognap me. My life would be ruined forever. No, I'd better not tell them.'

And when Frank wasn't reading books or on the internet he was asking the Trifles questions.

'Why didn't you use a titanium-zircon-based alloy when you constructed me? It would have made me much more heat- and weather-resistant.'

'To tell the truth, Frank, I didn't think of it,' Dr Trifle said. 'Besides, that old bucket and breadbox were just sitting here doing nothing.'

'Bucket and breadbox,' Frank said. 'Yes, I see.'

Or he'd ask Mrs Trifle, 'Why do your council workers always ask you what to do?'

'Well, someone has to tell them.'

'Why don't you put Melanie Mildew in charge of the road and garden workers and have Camilla run both the Council library and the school library? I could run all the meetings for you. I just read *The Master Guide to Corporate Council Meeting Strategies*. And I just did a Town Administration degree on the internet.'

'You amaze me, Frank,' Mrs Trifle said. 'You are the most useful invention that my husband ever invented.'

On Friday morning Dr and Mrs Trifle got out of bed and, as usual, a beautiful breakfast was on the table.

'I hope you don't mind,' Frank said, 'but I baked some little pastries for you. I also had some fresh fruit delivered. I put it on your credit card.'

'Frank, this is marvellous!' Dr Trifle said.

'Oh, and there's no reason to go to work today, Mrs Trifle.'

'No reason? But I'm the mayor.'

'Indeed, Madam, but I rang and organised things. I said that I was your personal assistant. The road crews will be fixing potholes near Mount Gumboot, the parks and gardens people will be pulling out lantana plants along Bogusville Creek, I've sacked three rubbish removal workers and told the other three to work twice as hard. Also the traffic wardens will be very busy today giving out parking tickets.'

'Parking tickets? What for?'

'I had parking meters put in all over Bogusville yesterday. This is the chance for Bogusville to make lots of money and catch up to Poshfield.'

'Well, yes, I suppose ...'

'And, as for you, Dr Trifle, I've finished your new invention. I made some improvements but I think you're still going to have problems with it. Why don't you both go away for the weekend? I'll look after the house and feed Selby.'

Dr and Mrs Trifle looked at each other.

'I guess that would be okay,' Mrs Trifle said.

'Well, there's nothing for us to do here,' Dr Trifle said.

'Oh, goody goody,' Selby thought. 'I'm about to have my own personal servant at last! This is great!'

And everything started off okay. Selby had Frank running around, cooking plates and plates of peanut prawns, and even giving him back rubs.

'Gently now, Frank,' Selby said. 'Remember, those are grabbers on your arms, not fingers.'

'Yes, Selby,' Frank said. 'By the way, about *Valley of Dead Souls*.'

'You read it?'

'I read all five books. It only took three and a half seconds. There's no way Dogboy could have killed the Gork king and found the Golden Glasses by decoding *The Chant of the Elves*.'

'Oh, great! Now you've spoiled the story for me.'

'Don't waste your time,' Frank said. 'Anyway, Dogboy dies in the end.'

'Frank! Why did you have to tell me that? How do you think that makes me feel?'

'I don't know because I don't have feelings myself. I don't have a human mind. All I can do is store information.'

'Well, don't worry about it,' Selby said. 'What you don't have, you'll never miss.'

Frank stopped rubbing Selby's back and then started again.

'Excuse me, Selby, but could you answer a question for me?'

'Sure.'

'You are a dog, are you not?'

'I am.'

'But you have a human mind and you know how to speak English and —'

'Whoa, Frank! Steady on. Okay, I'd better explain. I started off just a normal barking dog. Then one day many years ago I was watching TV and suddenly I could understand everything they were saying. It just happened. I don't know how.'

'Why don't you talk to the Trifles?'

'Because, Frank, if my secret gets out —'

'You'll become very famous because you're the only talking dog in Australia,' Frank said, interrupting him, 'and, perhaps, the world. And then people will be taking pictures of you all the time and they'll never leave you alone and you might be dognapped.'

'How did you know all that?'

'It's just like in the books,' Frank said. 'I read them all. You're the real Selby, aren't you?'

'Frank, you know too much,' Selby said, jumping to his feet. 'Listen here, you're a robot and you have to do what I say. You are never, ever allowed to tell anyone my secret, do you understand?'

'I'm not *your* robot, I'm Dr and Mrs Trifle's robot,' Frank said. 'I don't have to take orders from you.'

'I don't believe this!' Selby said. 'You're going to tell on me, aren't you?'

'I don't know. I might.'

'But, Frank, this is crazy! What does it matter to you? Don't tell me you want to make a lot of money out of me?'

'Money? No, I don't care about money,' Frank said. 'But we could make a deal. You have something I want.'

'What? I'll give you anything if you don't tell on me,' Selby said.

163

'You have a human brain.'

'You can't have it!' Selby screamed. 'Don't you get any ideas!'

'Calm down, my little canine friend. I just want to download some of your human qualities.'

'My what?'

'The things about your brain that let you feel things. I want to laugh and cry. I want to be creative.'

'Well, forget about it.'

'I can't, Selby, I simply can't. I've been emailing a fellow by the name of Professor Barking. Have you heard of him?' 🐾

'Yes, I have,' Selby said.

'He's been working on a way of downloading mind material from one person to another. I've made what I call a Brain Box based on his ideas,' Frank said, going into Dr Trifle's workroom and then coming out with a box that looked like the one on the cover of this book. 'I just want to capture some of your brain in here.'

'Get away from me!' Selby screamed, racing for the front door. 'You really are Frankenstein's

🐾 *Paw note: I met Professor Barking in the story 'Selby Unflips' in the book* Selby Sorcerer. S

monster!' Selby yelled. 'You're not putting my brain in that box! No way!'

'It's only your human qualities that I'm after. You'll still be a perfectly normal dog when I'm finished.'

Selby grabbed the door knob only to find that the door had been deadlocked.

'I don't want to be a normal dog,' he yelled, running for the back door. 'I just want to be me!'

'You'll still be you,' Frank said, coming after him. 'What are you worried about?'

Again the door was locked and suddenly Frank had Selby in a vice-like grip.

'Frank, you can tell my secret! You can do anything! But please don't drain my brain! I beg you!'

'It won't hurt a bit,' Frank said, as he strapped Selby into a chair. 'Trust me.'

Suddenly, Frank clamped a metal cap on Selby's head and, just as suddenly, he pulled the lever on the Brain Box.

There was a spark and a flash *Zzzzzzz zzzzzzzap*! and Selby felt a wave of energy flow through his head. In a second it was over.

'There, now,' Frank said. 'That didn't hurt, did it?'

Selby struggled to find words.

'Woof!' he barked finally.

'*Woof*? Did I hear you say *woof*?'

'*Woof woof*.'

'Well, fancy that,' Frank said. 'It worked. You're normal again. Now to make me human.'

Selby watched as Frank connected himself to the Brain Box and threw the switch in the other direction.

*Zzzzzzzzzzzzzap!*

'Oh, joy! Oh, joy, this is wonderful!' Frank screeched, as he disconnected himself from the Brain Box. 'Oh, Selby!' he said, kissing Selby. 'You are wonderful! I'll love you forever!'

For the rest of the day, Selby watched as Frank played music and danced around the house. He turned on the TV and laughed when things were funny and cried when they were sad. And he listened to someone talking on the radio and got very angry.

'That guy is right!' he exclaimed. 'They ought to line them all up and shoot them! What's wrong with our politicians?! Selby, I can feel things! I'm a person now. I can't wait to tell the Trifles. They're really going to love me.'

'Love?' Selby thought. 'What's that? Who are the Trifles?'

Selby went outside and lay by the swimming pool, his mind in a fog. Something had happened. What was it? Why did he feel the way he did? There seemed to be a new person in the house, a shiny person. His name was Frank. And those dog biscuits — they tasted okay but there was something about them. Something he couldn't quite remember.

Soon Frank came closer. He was humming.

'He's humming that song. I know that song but I can't remember where I've heard it before. Oh, I'm so confused.'

Suddenly Frank started singing the words:

*'Oh Dry-Mouth, oh Dry-Mouth oh wiggley woo*
*Dry and delicious so crunchy to chew*
*Fill up my bowl with my fave-ourite food*
*And if you do so, then I'll love you too.'*

And as he sang, Selby's scrambled brain began to clear.

It cleared.

And it cleared.

And it cleared some more.

'I think ... I think ... I know what ... what's happening,' he thought. 'And I know what I have to do.'

It was a stealthy paw that shot out into the robot's path. And it was a clumsy robot that fell over it and plunged straight into the swimming pool. Selby peered into the water and watched the flashing lights on Frank's chest suddenly stop.

Slowly the words formed in Selby's mouth.

'He tripped,' he said. 'I tripped him! *Yiiippppeeee!*'

An hour later Dr and Mrs Trifle arrived home.

'Frank?' Mrs Trifle called. 'Where's Frank? Selby's here but Frank has gone missing.'

'I think I just found him,' Dr Trifle said, coming in from the backyard. 'He's at the bottom of the pool. He must have fallen in.'

'Your marvellous invention! Aren't you going to get him out and fix him up?'

'I don't know,' Dr Trifle said. 'I'm not sure that we really want him.'

'I know what you mean,' Mrs Trifle said. 'He was getting a bit bossy. And I don't know that I like the things he did with the council. I may not be the best mayor in the world but I like the way I do things.'

'Yes, from now on, it'll just be the three of us around here,' Dr Trifle said, giving Selby a pat. 'You, me and Selby.'

'And that's the way I want it to be,' Selby thought, 'forever and ever and ever.'

# SELBY'S FINAL CHALLENGE

'Duncan Ball is coming to Bogusville,' Camilla Bonzer, the teacher-librarian at Bogusville Primary School said excitedly. 'It's Book Week and I've asked him to come and read his stories to the kids at my school.'

'Uh-oh. Here comes trouble,' thought Selby. 'I've got to make sure he doesn't come near me. Otherwise he might recognise me.'

'Who is it that's coming?' Mrs Trifle asked.

'You know. The author who writes the books about Selby, 🐾 the talking dog.'

'Oh, yes, I know those books ... well, a little.'

---

🐾 *Paw note: Camilla did say 'Selby' but of course Selby's not my real name.*

S

'I wonder if you could do me a big favour,' Camilla asked. 'Would you mind putting Duncan up in your house? The Bogusville Motel is booked out and I don't have any room at my place.'

'No, no, not here!' Selby thought. 'Anywhere but here! Please say no!'

'Yes,' Mrs Trifle said, 'I'd be happy to put him up. Dr Trifle and I will be out a lot of the time so I hope he won't mind looking after himself.'

'I'm sure he won't mind. But he really won't be alone anyway,' Camilla said, looking down at Selby. 'He'll have Selby to keep him company. In fact, I've always thought that Selby was quite a bit like the Selby in the books. Selby might even give him some story ideas.'

'Oh, no,' Selby thought. 'But hang on. What am I worried about? He's never actually seen me. The only times I've been with him I was wearing my dog-suit disguise. I'm just going to have to be extra-especially careful. One little slip-up and my life will be ruined forever. This is going to be a real challenge.'

★ ★ ★

Half an hour later, a dented and dusty car drove up and out stepped Duncan.

'It's a pleasure to meet a real live author,' Mrs Trifle said, shaking his hand.

'And it's a pleasure to meet a real live *mayor*,' Duncan said with a laugh. 'And a real live *inventor*, too. Pleased to meet you, Dr Trifle. Thank you so much for agreeing to put me up. And this must be Selby,' Duncan added. 'He looks very friendly.'

'He is,' Mrs Trifle said. 'And we love him to bits.'

Duncan bent down and, brushing some crumbs from Selby's mouth, gave him a good pat.

'Do you have a dog?' Dr Trifle asked.

'No, I've only got a cat. I was thinking of getting a dog but I was afraid that it would make Selby jealous.'

'Do you mean that there's a real Selby?' Mrs Trifle asked. 'A real talking dog that rings you up and tells you his stories and you just write them down? I thought he was just … made up.'

'Oh, no,' Duncan said. 'I could never make up such unbelievable stories.'

'So what is Selby like?' Mrs Trifle asked.

'All I know is that he's not too big and not too small and that he's a bitser — a bit of this and a bit of that. That's what he tells me, anyway,' Duncan said, looking at Selby's worn collar. 'What sort of dog is this guy?'

'We're not quite sure,' Mrs Trifle said. 'I guess he's like Selby — a bit of this and a bit of that.'

'He looks like a cross between a terrier and a pit bull. That would make him a terribull dog,' Duncan said and laughed. 'Get it? A terrier and a pit bull: *terribull*?'

'Oh, I get it,' Mrs Trifle said.

'Or maybe he's one of those dogs that looks for trousers.'

'There's a dog that looks for trousers?' Dr Trifle asked.

'Yes, a cross between a Newfoundland and a Dachsund, a New Found Dacks Hound. Get it?'

'Oh, no,' Selby thought. 'That's funny. But I've got to keep from laughing.'

'Hey,' Duncan said, staring at Selby. 'Did I just see a tiny smile on this guy's face?'

'Did you?' Mrs Trifle asked, looking at Selby, too.

'No, just kidding,' Duncan laughed.

'Those jokes sound like the dog jokes that our comedian friend, Gary Gaggs, 🐾 tells,' Mrs Trifle said. 'Like the one about the Christmas plant dog. It's a cross between a Pointer and a Setter — a *Pointsetter*.'

'It's interesting that you have a friend who's a comedian. Selby's owners, the Trifles, 🐾🐾 also have a friend who's a comedian,' Duncan said, taking a closer look at Selby. 'Do you suppose your dog, Selby, might be a talking dog?'

'A talking dog? I don't think so.'

'Of course if he was,' Duncan said, 'he'd be a cross between a Bloodhound and a Labrador. A *blab*-rador. Get it? A talking dog.'

'This is beginning to make me feel very uneasy,' Selby thought. 'I wish this guy would just get out of here.'

Suddenly Mrs Trifle looked at her watch.

'Look at the time!' she exclaimed. 'Drop your things in the spare bedroom. You're due at Bogusville Primary School in five minutes.'

---

🐾 Paw note:  She said 'Gary Gaggs' but, of course, that's not his real name.

🐾🐾    Which isn't their real name. (Are you with me?) S

---

'Thanks for reminding me,' Duncan said. 'Oh, and could I take Selby with me?'

'Selby? Certainly — but why?'

'I'm going to pretend to the kids that he's the real Selby,' Duncan said. 'Besides, they'll be much more interested in seeing a real live dog than a real live author.'

'Oh, no,' Selby thought. 'I'm going to have to be *super-duper* extra-especially careful.'

Duncan read Selby stories to the children all afternoon while Selby sat on a chair beside him.

'Selby here rings me up and tells me these stories,' Duncan said, 'and I just write them down. He says that he can't write them because he's a very slow typist. But, just between you and me,' Duncan added, looking over at Selby, 'he's a pathetic storyteller. I have to rewrite the stories to make them better. And I try to make them funnier, too. Selby can be a bit too serious.'

'He's smiling at me,' Selby thought. 'Everyone's looking at me. I'll just pretend I don't notice.'

'Is he really Selby, the talking dog?' a girl asked.

'I don't really know,' Duncan answered. 'He could be. Or maybe the real Selby is your dog.'

'But my dog is a girl-dog.'

'Selby could be a girl-dog. He made up the name Selby so that no one could find him. He also made up the name of the town he lives in and the names of his owners. So maybe he made up the fact that he's a boy-dog. Quite frankly, I can't tell when I talk to him on the phone if he's a girl-dog or a boy-dog. By the way, if any of you want to know if your dog is the real Selby all you have to do is remember the Seven Warning Signs of a Talking Dog. 🐾 Look for these things:

1. Reading material lying open near him.
2. His eyes secretly watching TV.
3. Look for a tiny smile on his lips when someone says something funny.
4. Cake crumbs on the chin are a dead giveaway.
5. If it's raining outside and he comes in with clean feet it means that he's wiped them on the mat.
6. His collar: see if it's worn out from being taken off all the time when no one's watching.

🐾 *Paw note: See these in the back of the book* Selby Screams.

S

177

**7. And look for an ear shooting up to hear what's being said in another room.'**

That evening, after dinner, Duncan took Selby for a walk. And as the two of them walked along the back roads of Bogusville, Duncan talked and talked.

'I'm going to hate to leave this town tomorrow, Selby,' he said. 'You're so lucky to live here. And you're so lucky to be with the Trifles. They're great. You must have the perfect life.'

'I do,' Selby thought. 'I do.'

'I don't know about being an author,' Duncan said. 'I mean it's okay but I'm getting tired of Selby's stories. I think I'll write my own from now on.'

'What is he on about?' Selby thought. 'When's the last time *he* walked up a glass building? When was *he* ever in a ship that hit an iceberg? When was *he* ever hunted by an Evil Genius? He can't come up with stories like that!'

'I mean sometimes I think I'm wasting my talent on stories about a talking dog,' Duncan continued. 'I could be writing intelligent books, books for grown-ups. I mean, honestly, some of the stories he tells me are so far-fetched that no one would believe them.'

'Oh, please,' Selby thought. 'Give me a break. This guy's head's as big as a watermelon. It's a wonder he can stand up straight.'

Duncan and Selby took a shortcut across a field and were about to cross a road.

'Careful,' Duncan said, 'car coming.'

Selby looked around. There was no car coming. In fact, there was no car anywhere in sight. Then he noticed that Duncan was smiling.

'Gotcha!' Duncan said. 'It's you, isn't it, Selby? You're the real Selby!'

Silence.

'You understood just what I said. You turned your head.'

More silence.

'Come on, I know it's you.'

Still more silence.

'It's not going to do you any good to play dumb,' Duncan said. 'You gave yourself away.'

'Okay, okay,' Selby blurted out. 'You caught me. I was afraid this would happen. Why did you suspect me? Was it because of the crumbs on my chin from Mrs Trifle's leftover birthday cake?'

'No.'

'Is it because my collar is worn from me taking it off all the time when no one's looking?'

'No.'

'Because I smiled when you told those jokes?'

'No.'

'Could you tell I was angry when you said you could tell better stories than me?'

'Nope.'

'Then how did you know?'

'I didn't. I just guessed. I've been to hundreds and hundreds of country towns and I've been with hundreds and hundreds of dogs. I often try to trick them. But you're the first dog that's fallen into my trap.'

'Oh,' Selby said. 'So now are you going to tell everyone?'

'Nope.'

'You're not? Why not?'

'If I tell people about you,' Duncan said, 'then they'll come looking for you. And they'll find you. And you'll become a major celebrity and everyone will forget about my books. Why read a book about a talking dog when you can talk to a real live talking dog?'

'You've got a point,' Selby said.

'So I want you to keep your secret a secret for as long as you can,' Duncan said. 'If you don't, then it'll ruin my life forever.'

'So you still want to write my stories?'

'Of course. What else would I write about? Nothing exciting ever happens to me,' Duncan said. 'You keep ringing me and I'll keep writing. Is it a deal?'

Selby put out his paw.

'It's a deal,' Selby said, shaking Duncan's hand. And then he added with a laugh, 'All this time I was scared that you'd find me and you finally did. But everything's okay. All the things I was scared of aren't going to happen. This is truly unbelievable!'

Author's note: Selby was right, this story is unbelievable — and I don't believe it. I've written it exactly the way Selby told it to me. I haven't changed a thing. And it's true that I've been to lots of schools in lots of country towns and, yes, I've tried to trick dogs into telling me they're Selby — but I don't ever remember one of them talking to me. I wouldn't be surprised if this whole story is just a trick to stop me trying to find out who Selby is and where he lives.

As far as I'm concerned, Selby has a lot more challenges ahead. And the search for Selby is still on . . .

# AFT

**After** you've read this book
you may wonder what really
happened when Duncan came to
Bogusville in that last story.
I can't believe he didn't remember me!
And I can't believe he thinks I
made it up! I mean I know he
was tired from lots of driving and
schools' visits and that but, well,
I'm beginning to wonder about him.
Maybe *his* brain is scrambled.
Anyway, thanks for reading
about my latest adventures. I hope
you had as good a time as I did.
Until next time — fill your days
with fun and have a great time!
CYA, Selby 🐾

x

182

# ABOUT THE AUTHOR

Duncan Ball is an Australian author best known for his popular books for children. Among his best-loved works are the books about Selby, the talking dog. *Selby Scrambled* is the twelfth collection of short stories about 'the only talking dog in Australia, and perhaps the world'. There is also a selection of stories taken from the other books, called *Selby's Selection*, and two collections of jokes, *Selby's Joke Book* and *Selby's Side-splitting Joke Book*.

Among Duncan's other books are the Emily Eyefinger series, about the adventures of a girl who was born with an eye on the end of her finger, and the comedy novels *Piggott Place* and

*Piggotts in Peril*, about the frustrations of twelve-year-old Bert Piggott forever struggling to get his family of ratbags and dreamers out of the trouble they constantly get themselves into.

Duncan lives in Sydney with his wife, Jill, and their cat, Jasper. There is a saying that dogs have owners and cats have slaves. In the Trifles' house it's sometimes hard to tell if Selby or the Trifles are really in charge. But in Duncan's house there can be little doubt — they are Jasper's slaves.

**For more information about Duncan and his books, see Selby's web site at:**
***www.harpercollins.com.au/selby***

# SELBY SNAPS!

Selby, the only talking dog in Australia and,
perhaps, the world, is back in the
snappiest collection of fur-raising and
fun-filled adventures yet!
So hold on tight as you rocket through
space and time with the perilous pooch
as he deals with a nasty knight and
an even nastier dragon!

And take a deep breath as Aunt Jetty
tears through town on a runaway
toilet leaving a trail of destruction;
then Selby is captured and taken away to
be the ruler of a mysterious jungle tribe;
and if that isn't enough he falls head
over heels in love with the most
gorgeous girl-dog he's ever seen!

But the big question is: will the world learn
that Selby can talk? Only you can
answer that question, so grab this eighth
collection of stories and read it,
and then scream at the top of your lungs:

I know the answer and I'm not telling!

# SELBY'S JOKE BOOK

Why did the golfer wear two pairs of undies?

In case he got a hole in one!

Why do brides cry at weddings? Because they never marry the best man!

**Warning!** Prepare to hold your sides and cry with laughter! Selby, the only talking dog in Australia and, perhaps, the world, is back with this fantastically funny collection of jokes and riddles and other hilarious stuff.

These are the jokes, folks!

What kind of paper is easily torn? Tearable paper!

A peanut went into a police station and said 'I've been a-salted!'

# PIGGOTT PLACE

*Duncan Ball*

*'Tell me what I should do with my life!' Bert wailed. 'Should I catch a boat to South America? Should I learn to play the trombone? Should I start an ostrich farm? I need your help! Give me a sign, any sign!'*

Sadly, Bert was talking to the only one he trusted in the whole world: Gazza, his stuffed goat. And, once again, the goat wasn't talking …

*Piggott Place* is a riotous but touching comedy about twelve-year-old Bert Piggott as he struggles to keep his family of dreamers, ratbags and scoundrels together. Everyone hates the Piggotts and now the council is going to evict them from their once beautiful mansion, Piggott Place. But the authorities haven't bargained on Bert and his young friend Antigone (would-be star of stage and screen) and their crazy scheme. The question is: can two kids take on a world of adults and win?

# PIGGOTTS IN PERIL

*Duncan Ball*

*Piggotts in Peril* begins with the shy and sensitive Bert Piggott accidentally finding the map to pirate treasure hidden many years ago by his great-great-great-great-grandfather. At first a quest for untold wealth seems the answer to all his problems but getting it means bringing along his scheming, ratbag family. Little does he know that what lies ahead are problems that even the pessimistic Bert could never imagine: the terror of turbulent seas aboard a 'borrowed' boat, capture by pirates, being marooned on the Isle of the Dead, and more.

*Piggotts in Peril* is a warm, adventure-comedy about the origins of the universe, the evolution of humankind — and pirate treasure.